NOBODY
KNOWS

KYRA LENNON

Michelle.
Thank you for your
support.
Kyra Lennon

Acknowledgements

Whenever I get to this point of publishing, the part where I get to thank all the amazing people who have helped me – I feel humbled by the kindness of my friends who have taken time out of their day to read, make suggestions, answer my questions, and help me shape my novel into the masterpiece (I hope!) it was meant to be.

Nobody deserves a bigger thank you than the exceptional Jolene Perry and Morgan Shamy. Jo, your belief in this story from the time it was a bit of a mess up until now has kept me going. Kept me *believing*. In spite of your always busy schedule, you still found the time to read, critique and advise AND answer my panicky, rambly emails when I doubted everything I wrote. I stand by what I said to you – one day we will meet in person and you will get the biggest hug you have ever had! And Morgan, your enthusiasm (and lack of notes!) was a huge boost as I battled the usual last minute publication nerves. I admire both you and Jolene more than I can ever express.

To my other fabulous CPs and beta readers; Annalisa Crawford, Clare Dugmore, Cassie Mae, Leigh Covington, Molly Williams, Elizabeth Seckman and Nick Wilford – your input and support is always appreciated!

The wonderful ladies at Concierge Literary Promotions – you have all been truly fantastic, and I appreciate the hard work you put in to the launch of Nobody Knows.

Ker Dukey – for allowing Nobody Knows a little space in one of your fantastic books, I am truly honoured.

Natalie Vanstone – for naming my fictional band within roughly thirty seconds after I'd spent days obsessing over it! I should have come to you first, right? Love ya!

Next, I want to thank my Fozzy Family – because, hey, if you're not rocking out with friends, what's the point?

Annalisa, if it weren't for you, I wouldn't have met any of the people listed below. I'd still be sitting at home, wondering "what if?" Thank you for accompanying me on my first adventure in years. That day will always be one of my favourite days ever, and it wouldn't have been anywhere near as much fun with anyone else.

Jess, I am so happy to have met you. I can always guarantee enormous amounts of laughter with you (and Jamie) – here's to many more gigs and carveries! (Oh, and the occasional bout of singing in the street!)

Natalie, Jay, Harriet, Amy, Emma, Matt, Neil, Penny and Bob - I loved hanging out with you SO much!

Chris, Rich, Frank, Billy and Paul – I wrote this book several years before I ever met you, however, it was seeing you live and meeting you all in person that inspired me to dust it off and publish it. Thanks for being the most genuine, talented, kickass band on the planet – Love ya!

Dedication

To Mum (and Dad)
for showing me what's important.

prologue
august 1997

I wedged my foot into a small gap in the wooden fence that ran around my back garden. I was a little too short to see over the top, and had to climb to peek at the boys next door. As I clambered up, I heard the sound of my jeans ripping at the knee. It was worth it though.

Not bad for a girl.

A skinny boy of eleven with scruffy blond hair bounced a basketball, while his older brother, a chubby, black-haired fourteen-year-old, tried to tackle him.

"Come on, Drew," the younger boy said, as he dribbled the ball just out of his brother's reach. "Get it!"

"I would if you'd give me a chance." Drew lunged forward, but not fast enough to stop his brother's shot being thrown straight into the hoop.

"Okay, Jason." Drew collected the bright orange basketball and threw it to his brother with a smile. "One more try. This time, I'm gonna get it."

"You wish."

Drew poised himself, waiting for an opportunity to tackle again. He followed Jason's every move but still couldn't get near. As he lunged for a second time, he

1

tripped, crashed in to his brother, and they both fell into one of the rose bushes around the edge of their garden.

A giggle escaped my lips, then my eyes widened as the boys noticed me. In panic at being spotted, I let go of the fence and fell backwards into my own garden, landing with a soft thud on the grass.

"Are you okay?"

The two boys, who had no need to climb the fence to see, looked down at me.

I nodded, too shocked to move.

"What were you doing?" Drew asked. His forehead wrinkled up, making him look like an old man. I thought he might shout at me.

"I..."

"What's your name?" Jason asked. His face was a lot friendlier.

"Ellie. My name is Ellie Hayes."

"I'm Jason. This is Drew. Want to come and play basketball?"

"She's too small to play with us," Drew said. "She won't reach the hoop."

"You might be bigger than me, but you can't reach it either," I muttered.

Jason laughed, a sparkle appearing in his green eyes. "Come on over."

Beaming, I ran to the gate, and he let me into his garden, where Drew sat hugging his knees on the wide steps leading down from the patio doors.

"Weren't you supposed to check with your mummy first?" Drew asked, in a way that probably should have made me uncomfortable.

I watched him closely. His shoulders were hunched and his foot tapped impatiently; his dark eyes gazed into the distance.

"Ignore him," Jason said. "Let's play basketball!"

Instead of joining him, I continued to stare curiously at Drew. This boy wasn't a mean teenager. Drew and Jason didn't have a mum anymore. Maybe he was thinking about her. Maybe he was sad she got ill and went to live in heaven. If my mum wasn't around, I would feel sad and sometimes say not *very nice things to people too.*

"*Do you want to play?*" *I asked, softly.*

Drew turned his head towards me, still with a wrinkle across his forehead.

"*He does want to.*" *Jason picked up the basketball.* "*Drew, come on!*"

After a moment or two, Drew visibly relaxed and stood up. "*Okay, I'll play.*"

chapter one
It's My Turn

"For years he's walked all over me, trying to get ahead. I snapped."

Snap.

I rose from my chair and began pacing, unsure whether to keep listening or throw my Jimmy Choos at the tiny backstage monitor.

"But what about that particular moment triggered your anger?" Danny Logan, the UK's top TV interviewer questioned. *"You were live on television on New Year's Eve and you had the crowd rocking. What caused you to turn on your brother like that?"*

Drew Brooks shifted awkwardly under Danny's stare. *"I saw him in front of me on the stage, getting all the glory, pretending he's the one behind our music. I couldn't take anymore. New Year was supposed to be a new start for us but he's still the same arrogant, selfish b... person he's always been."*

The sense of dread that had settled in my stomach since I found out this gimmick was going ahead had exploded into full-blown rage, and my temples throbbed with the tension. A few deep breaths eased the pain and I tuned out of the interview, unable to take anymore. I should have stayed at home, but no matter how much I hated this fabrication, I couldn't say no when Drew asked me to go along for support.

That's what best friends do, right?

The ten minutes before Drew entered the dressing room dragged on forever. When he stepped through the door sweat glistened on his face from the studio lights. My glare stopped him in his tracks. "I can't believe you went through with that."

"If I don't do as I'm told, I don't get paid." Drew gave a half-hearted attempt at a grin. My lips remained in a tight, thin line, and he sighed. "Come on, Ellie. What was I supposed to do? Go on TV and admit this is all a lie?"

"It's not all a lie, this stuff happened! This is your *life*. You can't blurt out years' worth of Jason's issues as if they didn't hurt you. This is dangerous, Drew."

"You're reading too much into it." Drew tugged a towel out of his bag and wiped the sweat from his face with slightly more vigour than necessary. "You knew I'd be asked about him tonight. That was the plan, remember?"

"The plan is for Derek to get rich by using your past as entertainment."

"If this works, we'll all benefit. Derek will finally get paid for putting up with us, and we'll get a real chance at making it in the music business."

Razes Hell's manager, Derek Richmond, was everything I hated. Not content with securing a much coveted spot on TV on New Year's Eve for the boys, he had to take it a step further and create controversy. *"You're in a rock band,"* he'd said. *"People expect this kind of explosive behaviour, and you have to give the people what they want."* Instead of letting them make their mark on the music industry through their talent, he'd dragged them down to his sleazy, get-rich-quick level.

Bloody stupid Derek.

"I don't care about Derek. I care about what this might do to you. When you were talking tonight… you didn't make that stuff up. Do you honestly think Jason won't see what I saw?"

"Why do you assume he watched?"

The note of bitterness in Drew's voice didn't pass me by, and his tone only proved my point. Whether he realised or not, after one week of Derek's scheme, Drew's well-buried resentment about always being the one to clean up Jason's messes had already risen to the surface. Although the New Year incident was as fake as a Page 3 model's boobs, the Brooks brothers had more than their fair share of crap to throw at each other, and Drew had just flung his first handful.

"It was still a risk," I said. "A stupid risk."

"Well, maybe it's my turn to be stupid. Maybe it's my turn to be selfish."

He shrugged off his shirt and pulled on a clean one. He'd actually dressed up for the occasion; he'd swapped his usual black t-shirts and jeans for… well… a black button-up shirt and jeans, but still, he'd made an effort.

My eyes lingered on his bare torso for a second. I tore my gaze away before I had chance to take in the light scattering of hair across his chest; his strong arms and his soft, slightly pudgy stomach that made his hugs infinitely more comfortable than being pressed against hard, ripped abs.

Okay, I took it all in and it annoyed me. There's nothing worse than swooning over someone you're angry with.

"So, what's the plan for tonight?" I asked, banishing *those* thoughts to the little compartment of my brain I'd kept especially for *those* thoughts since they first fluttered into my consciousness. Developing feelings for one of my oldest friends was right up there with moonwalking on the sun on my list of things I thought were Never. Gonna. Happen.

Yet there I stood, shamelessly ogling him with his shirt off.

"How would you feel about watching a movie in my hotel room?" Drew's question shook me from my thoughts.

"You promised to buy me dinner."

"I will buy you dinner, but in my room, not at a restaurant. Unless you *really* want to go out?"

His deep brown eyes flickered; a silent plea I wouldn't make him face the journalists who'd followed us around since we arrived in London. He wasn't used to the craziness of the spotlight yet, and I had more experience of being shunted out of the way by crazy fan girls than blinded by camera flashes.

"No. Room service and a bottle of wine is enough for me."

Actually, room service and wine was better. London had plenty of fantastic restaurants, but for a country girl like me, none of them compared to the quirky cafes back home in Cornwall. Plus, I didn't have to get dressed up to spend the evening in Drew's room. I could take off my one pair of trendy shoes that squished the life out of my toes, and slip into my trackie bottoms and a hoodie. Drew had seen me at various levels of disgustingness over the years; he wouldn't judge me for drinking wine in my lazy clothes.

Mainly because he still viewed me as the scabby-kneed kid who dropped into his life when I was seven years old, instead of the twenty-four-year-old woman who stood in front of him now.

Drew pulled me into a one-armed hug; a gesture of thanks for not pushing him to deal with his issues. I tilted my head to look up into his eyes. "You're welcome."

A small, appreciative smile crossed his lips. "Come on, Ells. Let's get out of here."

Flashy London hotel rooms shouldn't have been allowed to reach such low temperatures. With the heater on, and wearing a t-shirt, a baggy jumper, jeans and thick socks, I still couldn't get warm. Drew added to the frosty atmosphere, pacing around while he waited for Jason to join us… once he'd finished his drink in the bar, of course.

While we waited, I pulled out my sketchpad and some pencils from my bag.

I made my living as an artist, a job that gave me satisfaction in every way. My need to be creative made me too restless for a desk job, and the idea of a nine to five caused me to break out in a cold sweat. Once I gained my degree, I began to sell my work to art galleries in and around St. Ives. Shivers still broke out on my skin when I spotted my art in the window of harbour-side galleries, and my small amount of local success allowed me the luxury of taking a step back to work at my own pace.

I tapped my pencil against the blank page, waiting for the muse to strike; difficult since Drew's nervous energy zapped at my concentration. I should have been working on the first draft of some illustrations for a children's book; a story about a rabbit that gets lost in a supermarket. The thought of landing a job I'd wanted for so long made me giddy. Illustrating a children's book had been a dream of mine since childhood, when I used to illustrate my own, somewhat lame works of fiction. I hoped to be to a writer what Quentin Blake was to Roald Dahl. Of course, the chances of that were much slimmer if I couldn't make a damn bunny appear on the paper.

Instead, I began to sketch the outline of a face. With no-one in mind, I let my pencil do the work. As the face began to take shape – female, with huge curious eyes – there was a knock at the door.

As he strode into the room, he grinned. His long hair - dyed dark brown with purple highlights and hints of his natural blond at the roots - was tied back for once, and a crisp white shirt and black trousers clung to his slim frame. Unlike Drew, Jason thrived on his new popularity. Regardless of what Drew and I did, Jason had probably already called some of his city buddies to hit the town, as if his biggest screw-ups hadn't been exposed to the world. For the millionth time, I couldn't help but wonder how he and Drew could possibly be related.

Drew eyed his brother subtly, as if he didn't care whether Jason had watched the interview or not; his stance was way too rigid to be carefree.

"You okay?" Jason asked.

Drew gave a single nod. "Yeah. Did you watch?"

"Of course. I was only in the bar because it's cheaper than cracking open the fridge in my room, and you took forty minutes to get back here from the studio."

"Well, that's London for you." I placed my sketchpad on the bed.

"So, what did you think?"

"I think our album sales are about to go up again."

Money, money, money. No concern for his brother, no questions about how he felt.

"What? Didn't you think it went well?"

Across the room, Drew gave me an *'I told you so'* look, and I said, "Drew made the feud believable. But I still think the whole thing is a terrible idea."

A spectacular understatement. Every torturous incident Drew had mentioned during his interview had wrapped around us all, choking the life out of what we used to be and moulding us into the people we'd become. Somehow, we'd come through those rough spots, but this re-hashing of events we'd all rather have forgotten was a harsh and unwelcome reminder of the hell we'd been through.

"Relax, Ellie." Jason sat beside me and slung his arm around my shoulders. "We've got it under control."

Maybe he thought he had this under control; Drew most certainly didn't. I ducked out from under Jason's arm, and stared into the curious eyes I'd drawn. They didn't have the answers either, so I picked up a pencil and continued shading, bringing more life to her inquisitive features.

"Drew, did you ask Ellie about next week?"

"Not yet. I thought she might have had enough of us after today."

I lifted my head. "I've known you for seventeen years. I'm still here, aren't I?"

The smile Drew threw me awoke the butterflies in my stomach and I silently begged them to go back to sleep so I could speak.

"Crazy woman. Do you want to come to Scotland with us next week?"

I'd travelled around the UK and Ireland with the band many times. Each new place gave me a new experience, new inspirations to draw from. However, towards the end of last year work became my priority and I hadn't been on the road since mid-November. I itched to get back out with them. Travelling with my boys was one of my favourite things, and I refused to let some media fairy-tale change that. The only obstacle was my looming deadline. When I said so out loud, Jason scoffed. "I remember when you left your uni assignments until the night before they were due."

"Yes." I laughed, lightly clipping him around the ear. "Usually because you dragged me out to clubs every weekend when I should have been studying. But I didn't have bills to pay then."

"Oh, come on! Can't you pretend to be irresponsible for a couple of days? The only thing is... Derek wants Drew and me to travel separately in case anyone sees us together."

I blew out a breath. The whole divide and conquer idea was working out well for Derek. Divide the brothers, conquer the music industry.

"Where and when?" I asked.

"A small club in Glasgow on Thursday night. Derek reckons after this month and all the publicity we'll be playing bigger venues in no time."

"You'd better be."

"It's a means to an end, Ellie. Don't worry so much."

"Well, the end better come soon. Album sales aren't worth all this drama."

chapter two
Play That Funky Music, White Boys

Jason stared out of the cab window as we slowly rolled out of the airport car park towards the club Razes Hell would be playing at later. The rest of the band had been in Glasgow for a day already, since they drove the long journey in the band's van. I'd chosen to fly to Scotland with Jason for two reasons. The long journey in the van bored me senseless, plus I hadn't had much time to spend with him since Razes Hell's super fast rise to fame. We always used to travel together, the three of us, but since we'd been banned from touring in our usual way, I'd become piggy in the middle, bouncing back and forth between my two best friends; another unwelcome complication of this stupid situation.

"Are you okay?" I asked. "You're quiet today."

Jason turned to me with a smile. "I'm fine. Thinking about the interview I have to do in…" he looked down at his watch. "forty minutes. Hey, driver, can you step on it?"

The cab driver nodded but there wasn't much he could do with so many people trying to get out of the airport at once.

"Are you nervous?" I asked.

"No, but I've got to be careful not to slip up. I don't know what they'll ask. One mistake and this whole thing will be over."

He drummed his fingers on his thigh.

"How are you playing this? Are you supposed to be the poor, misunderstood rock star whose big brother holds a grudge against him? Or are you meant to be angry and hell bent on revenge?"

"Misunderstood. We need to keep the interest high, but also get some sympathy, too. Since Drew revealed pretty much everything I've ever done, I get to play the 'I've made mistakes but I'm so sorry' card."

"Are these your words or Derek's?"

He grinned. "What do you think? This is his invention. We're just his puppets."

Jason might have been amused, but I couldn't help wondering why Drew hadn't been given the same level of "training" about how to play *his* interview. Actually, I didn't need to guess. Similar to his place on stage when he performed, Drew got pushed to the back of Derek's priorities. Jason was the star, and *him* not fluffing his lines was way more important in his eyes.

"You don't have to be a puppet to be successful, you know?"

"Ellie, why do you hate this so much? Like I said the other day, all the drama is just a stepping stone to get us where we want to be." He reached for my hand and held on tight. "This will be over before you know it."

"Aren't you worried? You know how long it's taken for us all to

move on. This will be painful for you and Drew. *Especially* for Drew."
His eyes dulled and his shoulders slouched, making me feel guilty for
robbing the sparkle from his good mood with the reminder of
how badly he'd screwed up and how much Drew had done for him,
but his concern passed in seconds and he smiled again. "I'm not
worried, and you shouldn't be either. This isn't for you to worry
about. I know you don't want all this crap to blow up again. I don't
want that either, but we're stronger now. Stronger than we've
been in a long time. We can handle it. Please don't worry. Enjoy this
with us."

I wanted to. But then I remembered how angry Drew had gotten
on TV and how tense he'd been since, and that second of doubt that
flashed in Jason's eyes.

This couldn't end well. It couldn't.

"Whassup, Ellie."

"Hey, Mack."

I glanced around the Glasgow club's dressing room with interest.
The club's backstage area was a vast improvement on many of the
other places Razes Hell had played. Anything more than a few chairs
in the dressing room was considered a luxury, and this one had tea
and coffee making facilities, a vacuumed carpet, and - *bonus* - it didn't
smell of vomit. Jason booted me out of the cab we'd shared before
shooting off to his interview, and left me to navigate the unfamiliar
venue alone. I'd found Mack and Joey - Razes Hell's guitarists — on
the floor with several pieces of paper scattered in front of them.
They were in the process of figuring out which songs they wanted on
their second album and which to put on the backburner or scrap

completely. Watching them choose album tracks had an uncanny similarity to witnessing children fight over toys. Best to get out of the way before they started pulling each other's hair.

"Is Drew around?" I hovered in the doorway so as not to intrude on their selection process.

"He stepped out for some air," Joey said. "He won't be long." Unusual. If work had to be done, he'd normally be with his band mates, getting on with the job. I headed out to search for him, blinking as the darkness of the dingy bar messed with my vision. Drew definitely hadn't been out front when I arrived. The only people near the entrance were roadies and a group of fans huddled together against the biting wind. I spun around in a circle, and as if I'd performed some kind of Harry Potter-esque spell, Drew appeared, his large frame heading through the club towards me. A shiver ran across my skin as he approached in his ripped, faded jeans and a KISS t-shirt. He rubbed his exposed arms to warm them.

"Hi." I kept my expression perfectly neutral, as if seeing him had no effect on me whatsoever, although my pet butterflies stirred again. "Where have you been?"

"Out the back taking a breather. Do you wanna grab a drink?"

I nodded and sat down on a barstool, idly wondering why these places had to be so bleak. Black walls, black floor, dimmed lights above the bar so you can barely see your money when you pay for drinks. Being squished against sweaty strangers is awkward enough, and I'd accidentally groped more than one while searching for my purse in the dark.

"Everything okay?" I asked, as Drew leaned over and pulled out two bottles of water from under the counter.

"Yup." He handed one of the bottles to me.

His eyes told a different story. He hadn't been himself since his television appearance. I heard the frustration in his voice when we spoke on the phone, and I saw it on his face now.

Drew gripped his bottle with a firmness that made me want to trade places with it. Instead of unscrewing the lid, he pulled at the label, his fingers tugging until it peeled away.

I swallowed hard, glad he wasn't looking at me, and to take my mind off the way his strong hands deftly stripped his water bottle naked, I said, "How come you were hiding outside?"

"I wasn't hiding."

Heaving an impatient sigh, I jabbed a finger into Drew's side. He almost fell off his stool when he jumped away. "I came a long way to be here tonight. The least you can do is answer me in more than monosyllabic grunts!"

A smile tugged at the corners of his lips and the perma-wrinkle on his forehead disappeared. "Sorry. I had words with Derek and he pissed me off."

"He's here?"

"He's here. He wants to make sure we keep this feud going. He says we can't talk in public, and when we're playing, we have to ignore each other."

With Drew on drums and Jason on the mic, they never engaged much while on stage anyway so that wouldn't be a problem. Having to avoid public conversation was asking a lot though, since they usually spent so much time together.

I opened my mouth to speak but Drew held up his hand. "Yeah,

yeah. Before you say 'I told you so,'... don't."

"I wasn't-"

"Ellie. I know. You think we made a mistake and we never should have started this. I get it."

He turned away. One of Drew's best skills was shutting down from conversations he didn't want to have. I visualised one of those signs that hang on shop doors saying, *We are now closed for business.* His eyes seemed to do the same thing. *Go away, come back tomorrow.*

Placing my bottle of water on the bar, I said, "I'll be right back."

I hopped down from the stool and headed to the ladies room. Leaning against one of the clean white sinks, I let out a frustrated sigh. Drew's refusal to open up didn't come as a shock. He'd always been that way. His "keep quiet and hope the bad stuff goes away" approach had never served him well, though. There was only so long he could hold years' worth of pent up frustration inside before he exploded, cascading into a shower of rage and pain that threatened to drown us all.

It never used to hurt; Drew's unwillingness to talk about his problems. Another new, unfortunate side effect of my feelings. Another indication I felt way more for him than I allowed myself to admit, but I had to keep it inside my head.

Neither of you need the complication of a relationship right now. Get. Over. It.

I cupped my hands under the cold water tap and ducked forward to splash my warm cheeks. The great thing about alternative clubs was that nobody took much notice of appearances anyway, so it didn't matter that I now had a make-up free face. I grabbed some paper towels to dry off then went back to the bar.

As I passed the open front door of the club, the same group of people still waited outside, crowded together, shivering. Three girls dressed in skinny jeans and flimsy tops, and two equally under-dressed lads jumped up and down to keep warm. They'd obviously been out there a while in the below freezing temperature.

Hardcore fans.

When I rounded the corner, the band was preparing for a sound check, and instead of sitting down to listen, I stepped up onto the stage with them.

"Guys, there are some people outside freezing their genitalia off. Can't we let them in early?"

Drew shrugged. "I don't mind if they come in. You might want to check with the owner."

His gaze held mine, full of apology. I smiled, but before it fully connected, a pair of hands gripped my waist, causing me to spin around.

"Ellie, Ellie, Ellie! Lovely to see you!"

The feeling is not mutual. At all.

"Hi Derek." I faked a grin. "I wondered if we could let the fans come in early since it's colder than a penguin's arse outside."

"Absolutely. Anything for my favourite groupie!"

Urgh. He'd called me a groupie since he first met me four years ago. Twenty years old and shy, I hid behind Jason a lot back then. I'd explained numerous times I was a lifelong friend, not some random hanger-on, but he still continued to slap the label on me.

Derek scurried away to tend to my request and I stepped down from the stage and stood far back near the technicians, bracing myself for the explosion of noise. The sheer volume of a rock band playing to an almost empty room is enough to make a person's internal organs vibrate; I'd quickly learned not to stand too close to the stage or the speakers – oh, and to always have ear plugs. At my first sound check I'd felt as though my insides had been jolted with several thousand volts of electricity, and I'd spent the rest of the evening backstage trying to shake the ringing from my ears. Three days later the ring decreased to a dull hum, and vanished completely somewhere around day five.

Drew sat at his drum kit and the other guys took their places too. In turn, they checked their sound levels and asked for adjustments when necessary.

My eyes focused on Drew when he played. Being mesmerised by his talent wasn't new. The way he got caught up in the music always left me awestruck. Day to day, he was gentle and quiet; the second his drumsticks were in his hands, he transformed into a rock god, pounding the drums as if his world would stop turning if he didn't smash out every beat.

Passion. Drew had *passion*. Music was his biggest love, and fans who didn't bother to read the liner notes in their Razes Hell CDs had no idea he wrote most of the lyrics they loved. Drew never sought out the spotlight, but it irked me that he didn't get the credit he deserved.

The guys finished their sound check within fifteen minutes, and just when I thought they were done, Mack leaned into the microphone. "We need Jason back for the vocals."

"Nah," Joey said. "Everything's fine."

"Fine isn't good enough."

"We haven't got a vocalist to check how we all sound together. This will have to do."

"Derek will lose his shit if everything isn't perfect. Ellie." Mack turned his attention to me. "Tell him we need to do this right."

I glanced at Drew, who remained silent while the other two bickered, twirling his drumsticks between his fingers.

"Oh, for God's sake."

I didn't have any inner desire to be a rock chick, but my gut growled with hunger, and Mack and Joey could squabble for hours so I jogged across the room, perched my bum on the edge of the stage and swung my legs round then stepped up to the microphone. "Play that funky music white boys."

The guys exchanged looks of amusement, probably because I'd never done anything like this before. I sang in the shower, and in my work room at home. Those were my limits.

The opening bars of Def Leppard's *Pour Some Sugar On* me began. Razes Hell's cover was one of my favourites in their set, and their only cover amongst incredible originals. While the shy girl in me demanded to know what the hell I was doing, a small buzz of excitement shot through my veins.

I soon got into my groove, belting out the lyrics, and I hammed up my performance, wiggling my hips and shimmying my shoulders. Not normal Ellie behaviour, but we pretty much had the place to ourselves aside from some bar staff who weren't taking any notice of us.

Drew chuckled at my little show, and a moment of self-consciousness was followed by a moment of supreme, slightly bonkers confidence. I sidled towards to him and ran a hand softly down his cheek and along his jawline as I sang. My fingertips tingled from the sensation of his stubble and he laughed harder, one of his drumsticks dropping to the floor.

"You're such a dork," he said, shaking his head.

I gave his shoulder a playful shove, and he caught my wrist, his touch igniting a burning sensation on my skin.

Whoa.

Our eyes connected again and he smiled. It had been so long since he'd smiled like that - genuine, and without a trace of worry or stress – my heart flipped.

When Mack and Joey realised Drew and I had given up, they stopped playing, and a loud round of applause erupted from across the room. Derek had managed to let in the fans from outside, and to my embarrassment, they'd witnessed my horrendous singing. I gave a rushed curtsy, cheeks flaming, and hid behind Mack while Drew came out from behind his drums.

"Oh God," I whimpered. "Nobody was meant to hear!"

"Ah, you were great!" Mack said. "If we ever have to kick Jason out, we've got an instant replacement. You ready to get some food?"

In response, my stomach let out another rumble, and I nodded. "I think it's time."

I watched the gig with as much enthusiasm as ever. I'd heard the songs over and over, but no two performances were ever the same. The crowd made every show different, and the Glasgow kids were wild. Hands in the air, shouting out the lyrics, and girls trying to act cool in case Jason noticed them. *That* never changed. Without a doubt, he was always The One. Not Mack, with his shoulder-length blond hair and cute smile, or Joey with his deep blue eyes, or Drew with his intensity and sexy stubble. This amused me, because none of the girls who fantasised about Jason had any idea who he was. Truth be told, they probably weren't interested, they just wanted attention from a hot rock star. The soft features of his youth had been lost but his slightly rougher appearance seemed to make the fans want him more.

"Ellie! Ellie, where are you?"

My head snapped towards the stage. The audience looked around as if they could help find me, even though none of them knew me. I attempted to duck but Jason caught my eye.

"There you are!" He turned his attention back to the crowd. "Raise your hands if you were in here early for the sound check!"

The small group cheered and jumped up and down.

"I heard you got to see beautiful Ellie perform *Pour Some Sugar On Me*," Jason went on. When the students cheered again, he said, "Well, I'd like to see it too!"

I vigorously shook my head. Messing about in front of a couple of kids was one thing, but it was quite another to perform in front of people who actually wanted to hear a good singer.

"Come on up here, Ellie!"

He laughed as the crowd chanted my name. Everyone's eyes fell on me.

Think, Ellie, think! You're an artist, create an excuse!

Blinding panic froze my brain. If I didn't move I'd look lame, and the chants around me grew louder every second.

Oh, Christ.

I downed the last of my Bacardi and Coke, and the audience

cheered as I walked through the parted crowd. My legs shook with every step. My last time on stage was during a school play when I was eight years old. I'd gotten so nervous, I puked in the middle of a scene – and funnily enough – wasn't invited to star in any production ever again. Fine with me. Live performances were *not* my thing. The teasing after throwing up in front of my friends and all their families didn't stop until my first year of high school. I was labelled "Smelly Ellie" for three years. Jason had either forgotten about the incident, or assumed I'd gotten over it, which I definitely hadn't.

He took my hand to help me onto the stage and I stood awkwardly beside him while he addressed the crowd. A sea of expectant rock fanatics stared up at me.

"Don't worry," he whispered. "When the lights go out, you won't see them."

As the beat kicked in, I reminded myself to breathe and lose myself in the melody. Not easy to do when my heart hammered louder than the music.

We only had one microphone between us and as I waited to sing I stepped left and right - in a less funky version of The Carlton.

I made the huge mistake of looking out at the audience again. The lights didn't make them completely disappear, and in my nervousness, it appeared as though they were grinning up at me, faces resembling clown masks, ready to mock me when I failed.

Nerves took hold of me half way through the first line. Sickness clawed at my throat, choking me so the lyrics died in my mouth. The pressure, the lights; so much focus on me when I didn't belong on the stage, didn't belong in this crazy world of rock 'n' roll. The people below blurred and I blinked to clear my vision. No change; in fact, the masses swirled before me, my knees weakened and I ran off the stage and bolted to the backstage area before my legs gave out completely. Breathing hard, I barricaded myself against the dressing room door.

Nope. Sixteen years is not long enough to conquer my stage fright.

I had no clue how Drew and Jason had the courage to put themselves up for potential ridicule for a living. Once, I overheard some people openly mocking my work at a gallery and their words depressed me for weeks. I sure as hell couldn't handle harsh criticism every day of my life. Being on stage made me feel exposed, as if my less-than-skinny figure was an invitation for people to criticise, and even a single out-of-place hair would lead to trash talk. I wasn't particularly insecure about my appearance, but as someone who spent large amounts of time rocking a onesie while working on my next masterpiece, I couldn't cope with a job that put me in front of a live - often judgemental - audience.

I waited in the dressing room, jumping up and down to rid myself of tension until the boys filed in. The sound of the crowd indicated they hadn't been bothered by my freak out, but Jason pulled me into a tight hug the second he walked through the door.

Being crushed against a sweaty rock star didn't ease my annoyance. Well, not *this* rock star. I wanted Drew's comfort, his safety. His arms had been my safe place countless times; I never minded being crushed against *him* when he was sweaty after a show.

"Are you okay? I'm so sorry, Ellie. I was only having a bit of fun."

Typical Jason. Act first, think later.

"I didn't mean for that to happen, I thought-"

"No." I untangled myself from his arms. "You didn't think at all."

"Let me make it up to you." He cocked his eyebrow.

"Don't. You look like a deranged Bond villain."

"How else am I supposed to get you to forgive me?"

He didn't let up, and annoyance turned to laughter as he dragged me into another hug. Jason was hard to stay angry with, and that was saying something since he'd pushed and broken the boundaries more times than I cared to remember. As I released myself from his arms for a second time, I looked around for Drew. He sat clutching a bottle of water; a dark cloud had descended around him again. I recognised the expression of pent up rage on his face but knew better than to ask. He'd calm down in his own time, though how long it would be... well, that was anyone's guess.

chapter three
Too Young, Too Blonde

I sang to myself as I danced around my hotel room dressed only in a towel. The band always did something after a show; sometimes clubbing, sometimes a few drinks at the venue, and sometimes they gathered in one of their hotel rooms for a couple of beers. It was their way of winding down. Often, if I was with them, Drew skipped the partying and hung out with me. Like me, he had little interest in nightlife. For a break from the norm, I decided to join the guys at a club, and in spite of his mood, Drew agreed to come along too. Maybe several hours spent having fun would snap him out of his funk.

I pulled my chosen outfit for the evening from my suitcase; a short black skirt, and a black and white stripy top. Although I didn't often go out after gigs, I always packed suitable eveningwear just in case. An insecure person would have worried that wearing stripes when you're not built like a stick insect might be a mistake, but life's too short to live on salads when there's a whole world of chocolate to eat.

I ran a brush through my freshly dried hair and swung it over my shoulder, holding it in place with a hair tie. After applying some subtle make-up, I was all set. I grabbed my handbag and key card then headed towards Jason's hotel room. Our rooms were only a couple of doors apart and the sound of raised voices halted me.

I hadn't heard Jason and Drew argue in ages and my heart sank. Instead of letting them continue, I reached up to knock on the door to make them stop, but as I lifted my hand, Drew said, "This isn't only about us, though! Fighting between ourselves is one thing, but dragging other people into this crap is not okay."

"It wouldn't be forever. People will forget eventually and it won't matter who was involved."

"It matters now! For Christ's sake, we didn't start the band to make headlines on the front of crappy fucking tabloids! We started the band to make music."

"Without the headlines, people wouldn't know who we are."

"I'd rather be unknown and happy than famous and pissed off!"

"We should at least ask."

"No. It's not fair."

Whatever "it" was and who they needed to ask, I didn't like the sound of it. I rapped my knuckles against the door, shoving the argument out of my head, and Jason answered.

"Hi," he said with a smile. If I hadn't overheard them, I'd never have suspected they'd been yelling at each other.

Drew appeared behind his brother, and I said, "Are you ready?"

"Yeah. Let's go."

Two hours later I sat at a table on the club's second floor, watching as Jason wound himself around some random blonde on the dance floor – his argument with Drew obviously long forgotten. The girl couldn't have been much older than eighteen but Jason didn't seem too worried about that. He gave her a flash of his smile and leaned down to kiss her.

Funny. When I was her age, I was the one wrapped in his arms, kissing him. For a while, every time he visited me at uni, we finished the nights drunk and locked together at the lips. Because we'd grown up side by side, I thought we'd live the rest of our lives that way. Growing up, growing old together. Through my teen years Jason was the guy of my dreams and those visits from him, ending with a clumsy fumble on my bed, meant everything to me. But he had other girls. Girls who were willing to sleep with him without any kind of commitment, and I wasn't prepared to be one of them. I certainly had no intention of sharing him.

Then I met my first *real* love. Suddenly, everything I felt for Jason became clear. He was nothing more than a childish infatuation.

"Here you go." Drew disrupted my thoughts and handed me a white wine spritzer. As his fingers brushed mine, a spark shot through me.

"Thanks."

I hoped he didn't notice me awkwardly shuffle my stool away from his so I wouldn't spend all night jolting like I was being tasered every time he got too close.

Drew nodded his head towards the dance floor. "My brother has no self-control."

"Not true. He's still in the club. He hasn't whisked her away to his hotel room yet. I think he's showing amazing restraint."

"He hasn't had a girlfriend in a while. He must be getting desperate."

"Desperate? Look at her, she's gorgeous! Are you telling me you wouldn't have been interested if she threw herself at you?"

As soon as the words left my mouth, I realised I didn't need to ask.

"She's too young, too blonde, and I never hook up with random girls."

Just as well, really. I had to get over the bizarre glitch in my feelings that caused me to look at Drew in a whole new light before I could deal with him having a woman in his life. The sharp twinge hit me again. A painful clue this wasn't a glitch, and another harsh reminder I'd already been friend-zoned with no hope of release.

"Anyway," he went on, unaware of my discomfort, "I hardly think I'll meet the love of my life at a nightclub. Most of the girls here are only after one thing."

"You are the only man I've ever met who makes casual sex sound bad."

Drew slowly rotated his beer bottle in his hands, and I understood the reason for his silence. Just because he was happy to put on an incredible show with the band, didn't mean he would take advantage of the groupies. Drew didn't believe he *had* groupies; didn't think he could attract anyone, let alone have the confidence to indulge in meaningless sex with a stranger. His self-belief had been knocked out of him by his ex-girlfriend, Lisa. Lisa was a two-faced, self-involved wench, and for unknown reasons, she hated me on first sight. I figured she resented that I'd been in Drew's life for so much longer than she had. My theory went out the window the first time she showed her true colours. She used Drew's size as a way to cut him down, making digs about his weight then laughing it off but her malice was clear to me. Drew was over six feet tall with broad shoulders, of course he wasn't skinny, but certainly not fat. Even if he was, her snide remarks still wouldn't have been okay. The mere memory of the way she treated him made me want to seek her out and smack her in the teeth.

"Well, what about you? I don't see you down there getting groped by some random bloke."

My attention returned to Drew. "I'm not that kind of girl and you know it."

His eyes darkened. "You didn't have a problem with Jason groping you earlier."

Groping? When did...? Oh, do hugs count as groping now?

The way Drew looked at me over the top of his bottle, you'd think I spent my whole life whoring myself out to the nearest available male. In reality, Drew, Jason and the rest of the band were the only men I ever hung out with.

"First of all, Jason's not a stranger. And second, I don't recall any groping." When Drew only shrugged in response, I continued, "Is there something you want to talk about?"

"I'm fine." Drew swallowed down a large gulp of his beer. "Fine."

Even before I heard him arguing with Jason earlier I knew he wasn't fine. He hadn't been happy for a while, but that was no excuse for making me sound like a tramp for hugging someone I'd known forever. Lashing out was his least attractive quality, and thankfully, a side he didn't show too often. It stung that he used his defences with me, especially over something so stupid. Why would he care who "groped" me anyway? *He* didn't want to grope me.

Probably. But there *was* the time...

Stop. Now. We're not going over the three or four hundred times you thought he might have given you a second look, or maybe held onto you a bit too long after a hug. We're not, because you're friends. Just friends.

"Ells? I didn't mean to... I'm sorry. This thing with Jason. You were right. It's a bad idea. I don't want to fall out with you because of it, though."

I sighed. "I wish you would talk to me. Or to anyone."

"It's not that easy."

Not when you've spent your life building up a complex set of barriers to keep people out. He'd handed me the keys to open some of his doors, but I hadn't gotten close to unlocking them all. Most people eventually reached a point when they *had* to talk. Not Drew. He let everything pile on top of him, crushing him. Every day I was amazed he hadn't suffocated under the weight.

"I know, but I hate seeing you like this. All mopey."

He cracked a smile then placed his bottle on the table and took a deep breath. "So take my mind off my... mopey-ness. If you're not keen on dancing with strangers, how about dancing with your oldest friend?"

I grinned. "Old being the operative word."

"Oh, ha ha." Drew took my glass out of my hand and placed it beside his empty beer bottle. "Come on, let's hit the dance floor and pretend we're enjoying ourselves!"

After a while, Drew loosened up and his sour mood vanished. The heat from the flashing lights and all the thrashing bodies squished together on the dance floor caused my need for a little solitude to rush to the surface, and after an hour crammed against (mostly) strangers, I gestured to Drew that I was going to get a drink

"Did you see him? Did you see my brother on the telly? Fucking... Oof!"

What. The. Hell?

Jason swayed precariously on the bar, right in front of the barman who'd served him his last drink. Mid-way through whatever he was babbling on about, he'd slipped, tried to catch himself by grabbing an innocent bystander, and pulled the guy down with him as he fell to the floor.

"Get him out of here," the barman said. "Now."

Post-gig celebrations always seemed like such a brilliant idea at the time.

While Jason struggled to get up most people around him began to shuffle away from the crazy drunk man. Some of the crowd obviously recognised him because they were taking photos of him, ready to post on Twitter so the world could witness the latest drama as it unfolded.

Drew took hold of Jason's arm and pulled him up.

"What is wrong with you?" he snapped. "Act your age."

Jason's head wobbled in a comical way, like one of those nodding dogs people put in the back window of their cars. "I'm twenty-eight, not ninety-eight. Lighten the fuck up, will you?" He thrust his beer bottle at Drew's chest, spilling some on his shirt. "Here, have a drink."

Derek had said the boys weren't to converse in public, but I assumed fighting wasn't covered in that rule. I had only a split second to act before Drew lost it and the incident became front page news. Just because Derek wanted "explosive behaviour" didn't mean I had to let any more erupt. In fact, I was hell bent on extinguishing whatever I could and if Drew stayed where he was, the first real band skirmish would be on the Internet in seconds.

I grabbed his wrist. "Let me deal with him."

"I need to get him out of here," Drew snapped, shrugging me away. "Look at the state of him."

Jason chuckled, swaying unsteadily. "I'm fine. Fine and dandy."

"When you start talking like a bad country singer, you're not fine. Or *dandy*." I glanced around for Mack or Joey as the music seemed to grow louder and the lights appeared brighter. Excited clubbers could hardly believe their luck, and they were so close I heard the camera clicks from their mobile phones above the music. My palms were slick with sweat and my heart raced.

Thankfully, Mack spotted the commotion and weaved through the revellers towards us. "Everything okay?"

Drew opened his mouth to answer but I held my hand up, hoping the action would be enough to stop the outpour of rage threatening to spill from his lips. Anger radiated from him; toxic and a little intimidating but this was not the time for him to explode. Not in front of gossip-hungry witnesses.

"Mack, do me a favour and put Jason in a cab. And call Derek, he needs to know about this. Drew, come with me."

I didn't give either of them a chance to argue. I pulled Drew as far away from the scene as possible.

"What are you doing?" He fixed me with a death stare. "I need to make sure he gets back to the hotel."

"Why? Why do you *need* to?"

"Because if I don't he'll end up under a bus, Ellie!"

Instead of answering right away, I waited, watching him. My calmness set his teeth on edge, it always did. For several intense seconds, Drew's body grew rigid, not unlike the Incredible Hulk before his clothes rip and he turns green. Finally, I continued, "Mack's taking care of Jason. You don't need to ruin your night because he's pissed. He's a grown up. He can take care of himself."

"Look at the way he behaved tonight! What the hell is wrong with him? Can't we have one night out without him fucking embarrassing me?"

"It's late. You had a great gig, and he took the celebration too far. Let it go, Drew."

I didn't falter under his glare, and when he tried to push me away again, I held firm, my eyes focused on his.

"Dance with me," I said.

"What? No, I-"

"Please."

In the dark corner where we stood, away from prying eyes, I stared up at him and waited for him to calm down. Slowly, I loosened my grip on his wrist, and slipped my arms around his waist. When my hands rested on his back, his muscles relaxed beneath my fingertips and he stepped closer, pulling me into him.

Oh boy. Butterflies beat their wings inside me as his eyes softened and everything except us faded away. His hands on my back held me firmly and we began to move to our own rhythm, completely oblivious to the dance track playing around us.

I couldn't let it mean too much. I couldn't care that his fingers traced slow circles around the base of my spine, or that he shuffled his feet forward so he could hold me closer, tighter.

I couldn't care because this, him needing me, was only temporary. He needed me as a friend, and I needed to remember where I fit in his life.

"Why does he always do this, Ells?"

His question caused me to lift my head to look at him. "What do you mean?"

"You know what I mean."

I knew. Jason had always been the irresponsible one. He always had to take everything one step too far. While most teens engage in a little underage drinking now and again, Jason used to sneak into the house blind drunk, leaving Drew to cover for him. Instead of smoking a cigarette, Jason smoked pot – Drew had still never forgiven him for the time he got me high when I was at university.

"He does it because that's who he is. He enjoys taking risks, breaking the rules. When he gets an idea, he's unstoppable."

"Don't you ever get tired of defending him?"

Drew's body locked up again, and I loosened my arms a little and took a small step back. "I wasn't defending him, Drew. But you can't spend the rest of your life angry with him for being who he is. He's come a long way over the last two years."

Drew nodded slowly as my words sunk in. The distance in his eyes told me he had more to say, and after a couple of minutes' silence, he said, "I'm sorry I brought up Jason's cocaine addiction on TV."

"Is that why you've been so quiet since then?"

"Partly. I didn't mean to say so much, but everything came out, everything he did. I know he doesn't care if people know, but I do."

Because he's still your brother, and although he pisses you off, you still want to protect him. This was the world they'd gotten into, though. Whether Drew revealed his past or not, Jason's drug abuse would have filtered through to the public one way or another; that's how fame works. The more famous a person gets, the more scandal people want to hear. Especially if that person is a mysterious rock band front man.

"I'm worried about you too, Ellie. You're going to get pulled into this eventually. Especially if people find out what he did to your family." His head lowered. "And what he did to you."

My stomach clenched and I held Drew tighter again, just like I did the day it happened. I'd worked hard to push the incident out of my mind, and while I was certainly worried about what the fake feud would do to the boys, there was a hint of selfishness in my argument. Just because I forgave Jason didn't mean I wanted to be reminded of everything he put us through.

"I won't talk about it, Drew. No matter what happens. They could offer me a million pounds and my own private island with Chris Hemsworth as my personal slave, and I still wouldn't talk about it."

Drew cracked a smile. "Chris Hemsworth, huh? That's who does it for you?"

No. You do it for me.

Since I couldn't tell him out loud, I said, "All I want in a man is strength and a big-"

"Ellie, stop!"

"*Heart*!" I finished, laughing. "What did you think I was going to say?"

Drew grinned. "I never know with you."

Unsure what he meant and afraid to ask, I snuggled into him. Everything around us was alien, changing all the time. But in the moment, none of it mattered because we had each other. Safe in our own little cocoon.

chapter four
Cloudy With A Chance Of Storms

The first thing that happened when I turned my phone on after I stepped off the flight from Glasgow was the arrival of a text message from my sister, Lucy:

Don't panic, but buy a newspaper.

So obviously, I panicked.

I dragged my bag behind me, fighting my way through the unusually busy shopping area to get to the news stand. I knew *something* would be in the papers after the incident at the club but I didn't want to see it. The fact Lucy had told me to buy a paper meant only one thing. *I* was in the paper.

When I reached the newspaper stand, I was pleased to see we hadn't made the front page of Britain's best loved tabloids. I grabbed one from the shelf, and flicked to the entertainment section. The top of the page displayed a full colour photo of me running off stage under the headline *'Mystery Woman Razes Hell At Scottish Gig.'*

My eyes scanned the text; mostly it was a mini review of the gig, but the journalist had also posed the question of who I was, and if Jason and I were "just friends" based on him calling me beautiful.

Is that all it takes to make a headline?

I flipped through a couple of different newspapers to check what else had been said about me, but it was only more of the same. Nothing about Jason's drunken pratfall off the bar at the club.

As much as I loathed Derek, I'd never been able to fault his ability to quickly clean up a potential shit storm, though why he would when the shit storm was exactly what he wanted, I had no idea.

From inside my jeans pocket, my phone rang.

Jason.

He had taken an earlier flight, and Drew and Mack had gotten up earlier than the ass-crack of dawn to drive the van and equipment home. I'd flown back with Joey.

"Hey, Ellie. Okay, don't freak out -"

"I've seen the paper." I ducked my head, in case some eagle-eyed music fan recognised me from my debut as tabloid fodder. The picture of me wasn't a close-up, but even the small possibility of being spotted made me a little paranoid.

"Yeah, about that. I need to talk to you. Are you at home yet?"

His uneasy tone made me nervous. Of all people, I'd expected him to be the one making jokes and telling me it was no big deal.

"I'm at the airport. What's going on?"

"Derek called. Everyone's gone nuts about this story. He's kind of encouraged the idea that you... you're... part of the fight between Drew and me."

Sickness swirled in my gut. "What do you mean?"

"Some people think you might be a factor in why Drew suddenly hates me, and Derek said he'll make an official statement later."

That explained why Derek had halted the drunken bar story. Two brothers fighting? Interesting. Two brothers fighting over a woman? Priceless.

I knew only too well how the media could spin an innocent situation into something scandalous; you can't open a magazine or go online without the newest sensationalised celebrity story hitting you in the face, but it had never been a problem for me before. I stayed under the radar because, firstly, I never wanted to be in the spotlight, and secondly, I didn't want my career tangled up with the band's. I wanted to sell my work on my own merits, not because I had connections with famous people. Becoming successful by association would be tantamount to cheating.

"Tell him from me if he *encourages* this rumour any further, he can expect to find himself in court."

"Ellie-"

"No! I don't care what he has planned. I won't be any part of it."

My brain flicked back to the argument I'd overheard between Jason and Drew the night before.

Oh. Suddenly the truth behind the words they'd yelled at each other became clear.

Well, Drew was right. Dragging someone else into their publicity stunt was not okay. While Jason had always been a little selfish, he'd also been careful about keeping me out of the spotlight. This whole idea was juvenile and ridiculous, not to mention another slap in the face for Drew, who presumably I was supposed to have trampled over to get with Jason. I didn't ask for details. Didn't want them.

Whatever Derek the Dick had planned, I was shutting it down.

"Wait," I said, my mind reeling. "Did you know this was going to happen? Is that why you dragged me up on stage last night?"

Jason paused. "Not exactly. Derek asked us if you might want to help – his word, not mine. We're already doing better since New Year. People want to book us for TV appearances, and we've sold more albums this week than we did in the last six months."

"How is me getting between you and Drew helpful? And when have I ever come between you before?"

"You haven't. That's what makes you so perfect. We both know you'd never *really* come between us, so-"

"Are you seriously asking me to be a part of this?"

Another pause. "I think it would be good for the band."

"Okay, let me ask you again. This time I want to talk to the person who has been my best friend my whole life, not the one who thinks fame is more important than anything else."

"I don't think fame is more important, Ellie. I just didn't want to miss an opportunity."

"This isn't an opportunity for you! It's an opportunity for Derek to line his pockets!"

"Okay! You don't want to be a part of it. Fine. Sorry."

I let out a long, slow breath. He knew I'd never be involved in a lie. *Knew.* But when he wanted something, he'd go out of his way to make it happen. In some ways, I'd always admired that side of him. Without it he wouldn't have taken the band as far as he had. That side of him was also the thing that landed him in heaps of trouble, and *everything* about this plan screamed trouble.

When I got back to my flat I changed into some old clothes, cranked up the radio, and headed to my work room to paint.

The first thing I did when I moved in – before setting up my bedroom – was create a designated room for work. My art room became the one place I allowed myself to make a mess. Newspaper covered the wooden floor, and rough sketches were tacked to the walls. A huge stack of projects I'd yet to work on sat in the corner next to my easel, which usually held an unfinished piece of art. The walls were covered with grey smears since I had a tendency to jot ideas on them with a pencil then use an eraser to rub them off later. My work room also had a potter's wheel which I rarely used, but kept for days when I felt extra creative and needed to relax.

Actually, the real reason was because I wanted my Patrick Swayze/Demi Moore moment, but it hadn't happened.

Yet.

I worked slowly, unsure what to create. "Free painting" was an exercise I often used when stressed because it didn't involve the use of my brain. With watercolours and paintbrushes at my side, I painted random swirls and blobs while singing along to the radio. After a while, I lost myself in the melodies rather than the painting. As one of my favourite songs played, I put my paintbrush down and focused on singing instead. Beautiful lyrics always transported me far away from my worries, and I forgot about everything that had been bothering me since Jason's call.

As the second verse began, another voice joined in behind me. I spun around to find Drew in the doorway, grinning.

"If you're gonna sing that loud, you should consider locking your door."

"Jesus Christ." I covered my hammering heart with my hand. "You could have knocked!"

"I did. You didn't hear me, so I followed the sound of your voice and the smell of that cranberry stuff you use on your hair."

My cheeks grew hot. I could have sworn I'd locked the door, and if I'd been singing so loud I didn't hear his knock, half the building had probably suffered the sound of me wailing with the melody of a dying cat.

"Don't be sorry. You sounded good."

"What are you doing here?"

"I wanted to make sure you're okay. My brother's an idiot."

"Yeah. Sometimes he can be."

"I told him, Ells. I told him not to ask."

Drew leaned against the door frame, his expression somewhere between irritation and exhaustion.

Letting out a sigh, I went to him and let him envelope me in his arms. Wrapped in Drew's arms was one of my favourite places to be, joint first with my king-sized bed, except my bed didn't hug me back. Drew's hands on my waist made me shiver and I rested my head against his chest.

"How angry is Derek that I'm not getting involved?"

"He's okay. When Jason mentioned you threatened legal action, he quickly backtracked."

"I don't want my name dragged into this, Drew. I've got my own career to think of."

"You don't need to tell me. I know."

"Why didn't Jason consider that?"

"Because he's Jason. He's so busy trying to do what he thinks is best for the band, he doesn't think about anyone else. He's a selfish prick."

"He's not *that* bad. I just want him to consider what he's asking before steaming ahead and trampling on everyone around him."

"As I said, a selfish prick."

Right there. That was what I'd worried about since the feud started. It was obvious from Drew's mood that sooner or later the resentment would take over and he wouldn't be able to hold his anger in any longer. I refused to be pulled into a battle of petty name-calling though, even if Drew's words held a glimmer of truth.

"You need to stop." I shrugged free from his hold and turned towards the mess of a painting left unfinished on my easel. "If you really don't want me in the middle of all this, you need to stop talking right now."

I picked up my paintbrush and my hand swept black lightning bolts onto the paper, interspersed with the occasional cloud. It looked like a child's attempt at drawing the weather, but the point of the exercise was not to create a masterpiece. It was to use art to clear my head, and right then, my head space was cloudy with a chance of storms.

At least ten minutes passed before I checked whether Drew was still in the doorway. He hadn't made a sound, so perhaps he'd gone home while I smeared my frustration across the canvas.

He hadn't moved. He watched me from the exact position I'd left him in, his eyes a mixture of sad and tired, his lips set in a firm line.

"I miss your smile."

The words sort of came out of nowhere, but they were true. He'd always had this older-than-his-years look, but since the beginning of the year, his forehead had been almost permanently wrinkled, his mouth down-turned. The first time I saw him laugh in ages was during the Glasgow sound check, when I'd been mucking around on stage. His smile made his eyes shine and took away the impression he carried the weight of the world on his broad shoulders.

"Talk to me, Drew."

"I don't think you want to hear me."

I dropped my paintbrush carelessly on top of my paints and picked up an old rag to wipe my hands.

"I don't want to hear you tell me how selfish you think Jason is."

"Then there's nothing else to say."

He started to turn away, and I threw the paint-stained cloth on the floor, frustrated because I hated being part of this tug of war. Hated that the one time Drew wanted to open up, I pushed him away.

Hated that he didn't get how awkward it was to be stuck between my best friend and the man who consumed my thoughts.

"Wait."

"No, you're right." Drew headed for the door, forcing me to follow so I could hear him. "You can't be in the middle, which means I can't talk to you."

I grabbed his wrist. "Stop. Please."

His pulse pounded against my fingertips but I didn't loosen my grip. Instead, I held firm until the rise and fall of his shoulders slowed.

"I thought I could handle all this, but I can't. I've got more TV interviews next week, and I… I don't want to keep bringing up all the crap from the past. I never wanted any of this."

"Why you didn't say so before it started?"

"I thought it would be okay. I didn't expect to feel like this."

"Like what?"

"Like it's real."

Drew's eyes met mine with such heaviness behind them, the only thing I could think of to do was hug him. He didn't put his arms around me right away. When he did, he held me tightly, his chin rested on the top of my head.

I never knew it was possible to feel someone's pain through a hug before. Everywhere our bodies touched seemed to tingle with Drew's sadness, like some kind of emotional osmosis, and my chest ached for him.

What hurt one of us hurt us all – like The Three Musketeers, but with drums and guitars instead of swords.

"I don't hate him, Ells. I don't want you to think that."

"I never thought you did. I know why you feel the way you do, and I understand. Your whole life has revolved around Jason, but you underestimate yourself. You're not doing so badly."

He let go of me and slowly paced the hallway. "I know I'm lucky, but I've wasted so much time looking out for him, and when he hits rock bottom, he still comes out on top. If it was me, if I was the screw up, I wouldn't have what he has. He always lands on his feet."

I wrapped my arms around myself to replace the warmth lost when Drew moved away from me. "He lands on his feet *because* he has you. If you'd left him to go his own way, he would have kept on making mistakes. Maybe you should be proud of that instead of angry."

Drew shook his head. "I don't think you understand at all."

"So tell me."

He scrubbed his hands roughly through his hair. "I did, but like always, like everyone else, you're only focused on the end result, not all the shit I went through to get there."

"Hey." I caught his arm again to make him stop. "I was there too, remember? I watched you go through hell while you tried to help Jason, and I remember how much of a bastard he was to both of us, but what's the point in stewing over it?"

A bitter laugh escaped his lips. "I should have expected that from you. You were always out with him, getting drunk. It didn't help."

I flinched as his words flew out and hit me; as forceful and penetrating as spears stabbing through my chest. Drew was always only one touchy comment away from reminding me he was the adult and I was his brother's childish friend. It still hurt every time he pulled out that particular card. Did he think I didn't regret the "old days" when Jason and I got hammered most nights, and did stupid stuff like falling asleep in a drunken heap outside Jason's flat because we were too pissed to get through the door? It didn't take long for me to realise nursing hangovers and vomiting up last night's kebabs was *not* how I wanted to live my life.

"Getting drunk on a few nights out is hardly the crime of the century!" I snapped. "You weren't the only one who kept him out of trouble. The times I had to stop him getting into stupid, petty fights over spilled drinks. The times I wrestled drugs out of his hands! I sat with both of you when he was completely off his brain to be sure nothing bad happened to him. If anyone drove him to it, it was you! Always telling him he was being stupid. If you'd backed off, he might have figured things out for himself!"

Drew stared at me then his eyes closed. I knew I'd gone too far, but he had too. Just as I'd wanted to punch him in the face a second ago, I'd have done anything to take away the pain that kept him locked in the horrible place he couldn't forget.

"Do you ever blame yourself?" Drew asked. "Do you ever think you should have done more to stop Jason doing the things he did?"

I slid my hand down his arm and clasped my fingers around his. "Of course. But deep down I know there was nothing. They were *his* choices. What could I do to stop him?"

His voice dropped, and his eyes locked onto mine. "Nothing. Just like I couldn't do anything. It doesn't seem fair. We had the same chances, but he messed up and he still gets everything. It's the same with you."

"What is?"

"He was the one who dragged you up on stage and got you in the papers, and you still forgave him. All he has to do is smile, and you forget that he fucked up. You might think you care about us equally but you've always favoured Jason. Right from when we were kids."

Kids. That's all we were when we met, and Jason *was* my favourite Brooks brother back then. I adored him, because children don't want to hang around with people who never let loose and do something ridiculous just because. Jason was the person I had the most fun with, while Drew was serious and sensible. So many times he rolled his eyes when Jason and I built snowmen in the front yard or had water balloon fights in his garden. We'd walk through the house, drenched and giggling, and Drew would sigh at our immaturity. I wanted him to play but he always refused, always had more grown-up stuff to do. As I got older, I understood Drew had always carried extra responsibility, but now as adults, he still wouldn't let go of a time I had long since left behind me.

"When we were kids, Drew, you would barely give me the time of day. Of course I preferred him. Now-"

"What?"

I glanced down at our still joined hands.

"Things are different."

Following my gaze, he pulled away and stuffed his hands into his jeans pockets like a moody teenager. Thirty-one years old, and he'd morphed into a fourteen-year-old again. I wanted to pull his hand back, to be wrapped in his arms, or to run my fingers across his cheek the way I did in the club.

Without a coherent thought in my brain, I placed my hand on his face, then pressed my lips against his. Drew froze long enough to make my heart still, before his arms snaked around me. His mouth moved against mine slowly, like he wanted to savour every second.

Has he wanted this as long as I have?

The question had barely formed before he shoved me backwards away from his warmth.

"What the hell are you doing?" He stared at me as if I'd committed the worst crime ever.

A little shaken from being launched halfway down my hallway in his desperation to get me away from him, all I could do was blindly shake my head.

"I... I didn't mean to-"

"You didn't mean to kiss me? Then what *was* that? Your way of trying to make me feel better?"

"No! I-"

"If you'd listened to anything I said tonight, you wouldn't have done that." Drew kept his voice low. "I'm used to being second best, and I know I've always been second best with you, too. But you've never made me feel that way more than you have tonight."

My heart began a slow descent to my stomach. His accusation that I'd fuelled Jason's drug habit was a low blow, but it didn't cause half as much pain as realising I'd hurt him My insides withered under his gaze, making me ache in places I didn't know I had inside me. I couldn't stand it, the intensity in his eyes.

He took a step towards the door, his head lowered, and his slight movement scared me. I had to say something to make him stay, because if he left before I figured out what I wanted to tell him, the moment would pass and we'd both be too awkward to ever bring it up again.

Can't make this worse, Ellie. Whatever happens, things will never be the same.

I couldn't afford to stumble over my explanation. If I threw out words that weren't completely honest, I'd only hurt him more.

The kiss wasn't about wanting to make him feel better. It was about how he always protected me. How I felt his pain as if it was my own. How we both darted out of the club as soon as the coast was clear to go back to the hotel and watch a movie together.

It was about the man I'd grown up with, not the man who'd never grown up.

Still, the words wouldn't come out.

"I need to go home," Drew said. "We shouldn't leave things this way, but I don't know what else to do."

"Drew, wait."

"I can't, Ellie." He raised his head to look at me. "I can't."

This time, I knew I couldn't stop him, so when he opened the door I let him go. He didn't look back.

chapter five
It Had To Be Drew

I spent the rest of the evening curled up on my window seat, looking out over St. Ives Bay. In the dark of winter, the town was beautiful with the lights from the houses below, and the moonlight shining on the sea. I reached for my phone to call Drew at least ten times, but I didn't have a clue what to say. No matter how I rearranged the words in my head, I couldn't find the combination that would make him understand why I kissed him. I knew how his mind worked. He wouldn't believe me unless I gave him a specific date – rounded to the nearest hour – when I stopped having feelings for Jason, plus an exact breakdown of my thought process before my lips touched his. I didn't have that kind of explanation in me; that's not how it works.

But it's exactly how Drew works.

He was supremely obsessive about things that meant a lot to him. If he couldn't analyse and pick the situation apart until it made sense, it wasn't worth the risk. He'd lived his whole life that way. After his mum died, for a while he was the only one who could take care of Jason. Their dad did the best he could, but the loss of his wife crippled him. At twelve years old, Drew became responsible for more than any child should ever be, and learning how to weigh up consequences so young was something he'd never been able to shake. Instead of loosening up, the need to be in control, to protect himself and the people he loved had only got stronger.

Unfortunately, understanding him didn't make this any easier.

A knock at the door threw me out of my thoughts, and I glanced at the clock. A little past eleven. It had to be Drew. Nobody else would drop by so late. I untucked my legs from beneath me and ran to let him in.

When I opened the door, Drew made no move to come inside. He stood in the hall, hands in pockets, looking as confused as when he left. His hair was a dishevelled mess, and he was rocking his all-too-familiar furrowed brow.

But he's here. Maybe I didn't mess everything up. Relief mixed with a new wave of panic because this time... *this time* I had to find the words.

"Have you been out here all night?"

He shook his head. "I went for a drive. I knew you'd still be up."

"Do you want to come in?"

I opened the door wider and he came in, shoulders hunched. He obviously came back for a reason so I leaned against the door, taking slow breaths to calm myself while I waited.

A full five minutes passed, and neither of us spoke a word. An uncomfortable silence hung in the air as we focused our eyes on anything but each other. I found it increasingly difficult as the minutes ticked by because I wanted to stare at him. To take in every detail of his face in a way I'd never been able to do before. Or at least in a way I'd never fully allowed myself to do before.

Risking a quick glance, I caught him doing the same thing.

"Why'd you come back, Drew?"

"Why'd you kiss me, Ells?"

I straightened up, raking my hands through my hair to stop myself charging forward and kissing him again. Kissing was easier than talking.

He needed more from me. He *deserved* more.

"Not for the reason you think. I kissed you because I wanted to."

"Why? Why when you've always had a thing for Jason?"

"When we were kids."

Drew shook his head. "No. It went on for longer than that. Much longer."

"Drew, what do you actually know for sure about what happened between Jason and me?"

He shrugged. "I know you two were inseparable until you went to uni, and for a while after. And you're always messing around together. Last night he embarrassed you by trying to make you sing, and all he had to do was say a quick sorry before you started getting all huggy again."

His jaw clenched. Was he jealous? Was *that* what made him so quiet after the gig?

Duh, Ellie. He kissed you back, and he's freaked out. And you think he's *the idiot!*

With a sigh, I stepped forward and reached for his hand. He didn't close his fingers around mine, but he didn't pull away either. I led him

54

into the living room, and we sat down on the sofa. I let go of his hand as our bums hit the seat, but I stayed close to him.

"Drew, what I felt for Jason ended a long time ago. Yes, I thought I loved him once but it was young, don't-know-a-damn-thing-about-anything love. He was my first crush, and in the end it fizzled out the way most first crushes do."

"When?" Drew asked, his face still stony. "When did it fizzle out?"

"When I met Tom at uni."

"You must have still had feelings for Jason. You don't just fall out of love with someone. Feelings don't go away overnight."

Oh.

I wasn't only dealing with his insecurity about his brother. Clearly, while he'd been driving around, he'd dug up the other painful memory he usually kept buried deep. Lisa. The cold-hearted bitch who made his life a misery.

She broke him, and when he started to heal, Jason broke him again.

I couldn't change the past. Couldn't erase the fact I once had a thing for Jason, or wipe away the pain Drew still carried around about the way Lisa treated him. She'd left so many scars. Scars the next woman in his life would have to work hard to heal. Even knowing as much about Drew as I did, I had no idea where to begin but I wanted to try.

"I don't think I can ever explain in a way that will be enough for you. Maybe that's why I kissed you. Because I didn't think you'd believe me any other way."

"So you did it to prove a point," he said, standing up. "You say you don't feel anything for Jason, but last night you were… you two were…" he stopped, shaking his head, his jaw clenching again as if the mere memory of Jason hugging me made him want to put his fist through a wall.

My insides fizzed with hope. I thought I'd been in this thing alone. His reaction over something so insignificant suggested otherwise, but I couldn't let myself get too carried away yet. Not until I was sure he was in the same place as me.

"It was a hug, Drew. You've seen us hugging a million times."

And I felt more in the five seconds I touched your cheek than I did in the few minutes I was with Jason.

"Yeah. Well, now it bothers me." He wearily rubbed his hand across his forehead, turning away. "I didn't want to get into this with you, Ells. It's too complicated."

"What is?"

"This. You. Me. I can't handle it."

"Why not?"

He spun around to face me. "Aren't you afraid of what might happen?"

His shoulders were tense and I ached to go to him and ease it away. I got why he was so scared but he hadn't given me anything to hold on to. Nothing to tell me exactly how he felt when I kissed him, or what he'd been thinking, or why he came back.

"I'm more afraid of what will happen if we don't talk about this."

"I don't know where to start. I don't remember when I started to…" he paused, suddenly twitchier than Jason used to get after a hit. He pulled at his sleeves, and I hated that he was so uncomfortable, but I wouldn't let him sidestep the conversation. He forced me to talk, now it was his turn.

He sighed. "I'm not good at this."

"Can you try? Please?"

Drew turned to me, his gaze softening. "I've wanted you to look at me the way you looked at Jason for so long. Now you are, and I don't know if I can act on it."

"Why not?"

"Because I don't want to be second best, Ells. Not with you."

I stared into his eyes, willing him to understand. Willing him to push aside his fears. When I was sure the truth was seeping into his brain, I stood up and reached for his hand, but pulled back, afraid of moving too fast, of messing things up before they started.

A thundering beat pounded in my chest, and Drew stepped forward, gently resting his hand on my cheek. With his other hand, he pulled me to him, closing the gap between us. The simple gesture of him stroking my cheek shouldn't have affected me so much, but it sent a shiver through me, and when his lips met mine and he buried his hand in my hair, everything around me disappeared.

God, his kiss was intense. Soft and slow, but every brush of his lips told me how much he wanted this, maybe for even longer than I had. My arms circled around his waist and it took every ounce of strength I had not to whimper. For a big guy, his touch was so gentle. His fingers moved in little circles across my lower back, the way they had when we danced, shooting sparks up and down my spine.

chapter six

Shut Up And Kiss Me

When I woke up, I could smell Drew on me. On the clothes I'd fallen asleep in. He didn't stay. He'd covered me with a blanket, and left me a note with three simple words.

See you tonight x

Those words set my head spinning. My insides swirled with nerves, which was ridiculous considering I'd known him forever and never been nervous around him before. But this was different. We were about to have our first official date. Granted, it was going to be at my flat because we were nowhere near ready to go public with our relationship yet, but it was still a big deal. Drew said if we couldn't go out, he would bring a romantic restaurant experience to me. Well, he never said "romantic". Romance is kind of implied on a first date, though, right?

We'd spent a lot of time talking the night before, wrapped up in each other. His arms circled around me; me leaning back against his chest, occasionally tilting my head for more kisses. There was a long way to go before the ghost of Jason was chased away forever, I understood that. One magical evening wouldn't fix Drew's insecurities. It wasn't a guarantee of a happy ever after. It was a beginning. A promise to find our way through the mess together.

There's a belief an artist can make beautiful creations out of anything. I was the definite exception to the rule. I thought I had some cloth napkins tucked away somewhere, but all I found in my cupboard was leftover paper Christmas napkins, frosty blue with cartoon elves on them. Not ideal for a romantic dinner, but they'd have to do. After spending more than an hour on the internet, trying to work out how to fold them into swans so the Christmas patterns wouldn't be as obvious, I gave up and folded the squares in half to make triangles.

Uber creative.

I was a little behind schedule since I'd spent the afternoon perfecting and submitting my bunny to the publisher, and then faffing around with the napkins, so I showered quickly, and slipped into my sexiest underwear. There was no chance of Drew seeing my underwear yet – probably – but every girl feels more confident wearing her finest lingerie. I needed any extra confidence I could muster because nerves had taken hold of me in a big way.

I'd imagined a first date with Drew on the rare occasions I opened the *Stop Thinking About Him* compartment of my brain. I imagined I would feel excited, but I hadn't counted on nerves rattling around me too. The night before, we'd crossed the friendship line. We were about to take another leap, and what if he changed his mind? What if

Drew decided he was wrong, and couldn't take such a huge gamble on us?

I rooted through my wardrobe until I found the item I was looking for; my black, knee length dress with full skirt that flared out at the hips. Perfect. The straps of the dress resembled belts with buckles, and although I deemed it the trendiest item of clothing in my wardrobe, I'd never worn it before. Once I was dressed, I set to work curling my hair, and added a little make-up.

When Drew arrived, the candles were lit, the lights were low, mood music played in the background, and my stomach turned over in a way it hadn't done in years.

Butterflies because of my best friend. So. Weird.

I opened the door and greeted Drew with a smile that may have looked fake. *Damn nerves.*

I'd seen him dressed up on many occasions, but this was the first time he made me breathless. Black trousers, a blue shirt, and carrying two bags full of ingredients to make dinner.

He *definitely* hadn't changed his mind about us. He'd never looked hotter.

"Hey you."

Drew smiled, his brown eyes connecting with mine. "You look amazing."

"So do you."

We stood awkwardly in the doorway and Drew said, "Are you going to let me in?"

"Yes, sorry." I shifted out of the way so he could step inside. "I was just hoping my tummy would stop acting crazy."

An uncharacteristic blush crossed Drew's cheeks. "We can probably work through that together."

Watching Drew cook in my kitchen, wearing my pink apron to keep his shirt clean, was almost as much fun as eating the meal. He made his famous lasagne, complete with homemade sauce. There was something bizarre about seeing a well-dressed rock star preparing dinner. Surely there were some rules of coolness he was breaking by being so domesticated? He could have at least brought a dessert to flambé so he had something to set fire to.

The food was incredible. I wouldn't usually have eaten so much on a first date, but I figured it was okay to break that particular rule since we'd been friends for so long. Besides, since Drew had gone to so much effort, it would have been rude not to finish the entire dish. We sat at my Christmas-themed table, holding hands, the conversation flowing as easily as the wine.

"Will you dance with me, Ells?"

The gentle sounds of Sinatra played, and although I'd eaten so much I could barely move, I didn't have to try too hard to muster enough energy for a slow dance.

I held him close, my head resting against his chest. I loved it there; breathing him in, hearing his heartbeat pounding as hard as mine. He wasn't one of those guys who drowned himself in cologne. In fact, he rarely wore cologne at all. Drew smelled like the ocean; cool, powerful. Unless he'd been on stage, when he smelled of sweat, and his hands held the woody aroma of his drumsticks. Either way, the scent of him comforted me, *excited* me.

This was so different from when we danced together at the club. That night was filled with tension, even after I'd calmed him down. Now the tension was different. Aroused instead of angry, both anticipating what would happen next.

"What are you thinking about, Ells?" Drew asked, his hands sliding down to my hips.

"Us. How good it feels to be on a date with you. How much better it is now I don't have to pretend or hide my feelings anymore."

I hadn't been aware of tension in Drew's body but as I spoke, his muscles loosened beneath my fingers and he pulled me in tighter, as if my words were everything he needed to hear.

He kissed the top of my head. "I didn't think we'd ever get here."

"I didn't think you wanted to."

He laughed softly. "I didn't think *you* wanted to."

"Well, aren't we a pair of idiots." I grinned at him, and he closed his eyes, resting a hand on my cheek.

"You were so worth waiting for, Ellie."

I loved this side of him. The I-can't-imagine-being-anywhere-else side. Even so, I couldn't resist teasing him. "You are the cheesiest rock star ever."

Drew opened his eyes, raising an eyebrow. "Oh really?"

"Really."

Without warning, he lifted me off the ground. He crushed his mouth against mine, knocking the breath out of me for the second time that evening. My legs clamped around his waist, my arms around his neck. His fingers moved up and down my spine, unknowingly following the tingles he'd created as his lips claimed mine.

"Still think I'm cheesy?" he asked, his breath hot on my neck.

"Shut up and kiss me."

Drew laughed and granted my request. I pressed myself into him, loving how easy it was to switch from joking around to... this. As his tongue slid into my mouth, my fingers delved into his hair, curling it between my fingers. The wine on his lips was a million times more intoxicating than if I'd drank the whole bottle myself, and the brush of his stubble against my cheek shot my senses into overdrive. I trembled from the intensity, the long-suppressed desire, and before I could stop it, a small moan escaped me.

Drew stopped, mid-kiss, and I froze, hoping he'd breeze past the moment and go back to tormenting me with his lips.

"Ellie, what was that?"

Dammit.

I didn't answer, instead I tried to kiss him again but he leaned back, laughing. I unclenched my legs from his waist and dropped to the floor, hiding the blush on my cheeks by burying my face into his shoulder.

Ah, he smells so good! My body was on sensory overload.

"I've never heard you make that sound before," he teased. I gave his hair a playful tug.

"I bet you're pleased with yourself now, aren't you? You made me moan like a porn star."

He gathered me into him. "Ells, come on. You don't think I feel that way, too?"

"I know you do, but you didn't embarrass yourself!"

"Don't be embarrassed, it was sexy as hell. I only laughed because I was surprised."

"Why?"

"Because I didn't realise I made *you* feel that way."

Really? My underwear is vibrating with the urge to pop off so you can touch me properly.

The voice telling him he wasn't good enough was still loud and clear, reminding me how far I had to go to make him understand.

And it was that part of me that knew it was too soon for us to go any further yet.

"Drew, I've waited a long time to be here with you. But this… wanting you this much… it's new for me too. You *do* make me feel that way, though. More than I can tell you. Which… erm… explains the moaning."

Drew laughed softly, before leaning down to brush his lips against mine. "Want to finish our dance?"

I nodded. "I'd love to."

chapter seven

My Shriek Probably Deafened

Several Dogs

Not gonna lie, sneaking around with Drew was hard. We'd decided against telling anyone we were together for the time being. What we had was so new. We weren't only trying to avoid another media storm, we were adjusting to a huge change in our relationship. Involving anyone else, even our closest friends and families, was too big a step. Keeping our relationship under wraps was something we needed to do for a while, to protect it, nurture it before we let anyone else in.

After our first date, all we wanted was to spend more time together. With Drew having to disappear for interviews since Razes Hell's album reached the Top 20 in the download charts, and me working through some of my unfinished projects, time alone was scarce. An opportunity to be together presented itself a little over a week after our first date. Instead of cancelling their remaining small gigs, the band chose to honour them before taking time out to get their next album recorded, and bigger venues booked. Drew asked if I wanted to go to London with them for their final pub show; a farewell to their old life before the new one began.

It couldn't have been clearer how glad Jason was to be saying goodbye to the pub scene. Drew, however, would miss the simplicity. I knew there was a big part of him that didn't want their career to change, and I couldn't help feeling the same way. I was thrilled about their success, but Drew and I had *just* got together, and no matter how much freedom my job gave me, I wouldn't be able to travel with them once they were on the road more often. There are only so many art supplies you can fit in a suitcase.

My phone buzzed across the bedside table in my hotel room, and I sat up. The number was unfamiliar, but I answered anyway.

"Is that Ellie Hayes?"

The professional sounding female voice surprised me. I'd expected one of those annoying recorded messages, telling me I'd won a holiday.

"Yes, this is Ellie."

"I'm Jayne Black, author of *'Where Are You, Grey Rabbit?'*"

My mouth went dry. *Oh, God. She's calling me. And she sounds happy.*

"Uh… I… wow. It's great to hear from you."

"I have some news for you. I had a lot of illustrations to choose from, and picking my favourite wasn't easy but your sketches were the ones I kept coming back to. Ellie, I'd love for you to illustrate the book."

My shriek probably deafened several dogs, not to mention the woman who was about to employ me, but I couldn't help myself. I'd waited so long for an opportunity this big; I never expected to be chosen on my first attempt.

"Oh, God. Sorry for screaming in your ear! Thank you. Thank you so much."

Jayne laughed. "If I can expect this level of enthusiasm in everything you do, I'm sure we'll get along brilliantly."

"I guarantee it." She must have heard the smile in my voice. The Cheshire Cat had nothing on me.

"I'll email all the details and the contract to you in the morning. If you have any questions, please tell me and I'll do my best to answer them."

"Okay. Thanks again, Jayne. This is amazing. You're amazing!"

She laughed again. "I'll look forward to hearing from you soon, and thank you, Ellie. Your work is wonderful."

"Thank you."

As I hung up the phone, I tried to calculate exactly how many times I'd thanked her, but then the realisation set in. I was about to become an illustrator! I slipped my phone into my pocket, and galloped – Miranda style – around the room.

Drew. I had to tell Drew.

I was so ready to pounce on him that when Jason opened Drew's door, my body did a weird backwards jolt thing, making me look like I was having a seizure.

"Hey Ellie," he said, as I struggled to remove the surprise from my face. "We're heading out in a few minutes, but come in."

Drew looked up from the notes on his lap and smiled in the special way he reserved for me. It had only been three days since we last saw each other, but my breath hitched in anticipation of having some alone time with him later.

"I have news. The author of the bunny book called. I got the illustrator job!"

I bounced up and down on the spot, and Jason launched himself at me.

"Congratulations! I know how long you've wanted this."

He did, too. Possibly even more than Drew. He was the one I showed my work to when I was younger, getting his opinions on which of my drawings would look good in a book.

I was such a dorky kid.

And when we grew up, many drunken nights ended with us sharing our plans for the future. It was pretty amazing two of our biggest dreams had come true at the exact same time.

"Thank you." I hugged him tightly.

"I'm proud of you, Ellie. You did it."

"We both did it!"

I pulled back a little to smile at my best friend. We'd come a long way since the days when it seemed as though the dreams we had would always be out of reach.

"Can I get a hug with the superstar now?"

Jason let me go and Drew bundled me into his arms. I tried not to give a pathetic sigh of joy as I breathed him in. "You two are the superstars."

"Not today. Today is all about you. This is amazing, Ells."

"It's only a small publication."

"So? It's still a book that'll have your name in, and who knows what that could lead to?"

"Not to break up the hug-fest," Jason said, "but we need to go."

Drew glanced down at his watch, one arm still around me. "Yeah, you're right."

"I'm gonna go grab the rest of the new song lyrics from my room. I'll meet you downstairs in ten." He fixed me with a grin. "Congratulations again, Ellie."

When Jason left, Drew lifted me up and spun me around in a circle before pressing me against the door. "God, I've missed you." His lips met mine in a way that somehow managed to be both sweet and romantic, and hot as hell, not giving me a chance to tell him I'd missed him, too. The awkwardness we'd had on our first date faded more with every kiss – and there had been a *lot* of kisses. Drew gently stroked my cheek with his thumb. "I wish I didn't have to leave you already."

"Me too. But you've got a show to prepare for."

"You wanna come with us? We won't get much time alone, but… this is a big day for you, Ells. I hate to think of you sitting in your room instead of celebrating."

I loved how much he got it. How he knew being stuck in a hotel room when I wanted to jump around screaming with joy was my idea of a nightmare. How he knew exactly how much the job meant to me, even without being the one I'd divulged my childhood dreams to.

"It's okay." I brushed my lips against his. "We'll celebrate later. Your full attention should be on the band today."

He let out a small groan. "Can't I pretend to be ill?" His fingers pressed into my hips, drawing me closer.

I could so easily have given in. Not seeing him for a few days, the way he touched me, the way his eyes never left mine – I wanted him to stay.

69

But I didn't want our first time to be a quickie up against his hotel room door.

"No." I laughed, lacing our fingers together. "You have to go. But believe me, if I had a choice, I'd spend the whole day in here with you instead of trying to hide what we are."

Drew brought my hand to his lips, but a slight frown crossed his face. "You are okay with keeping this a secret, aren't you? I mean, we agreed it was best."

"Yeah. For now. I hate lying to everyone, but this is what's right for us."

"Are you worried about Jason?"

A ripple of dread shimmied across my skin. I'd anticipated that Drew wouldn't let his issues with Jason fade easily into the background. Letting go had never been his strong point.

But I *was* worried. Both of the guys had witnessed every significant moment in my life, sometimes before my family, so keeping Jason in the dark about me and Drew felt unnatural and wrong.

"Yes, I'm worried. We've never kept secrets from him before."

He nodded, and from the way his face clouded over, I could tell I'd cracked open the door to his insecurities again.

"I know. I…" he paused, shaking his head. "Never mind."

"Tell me."

"Forget it." He stepped away but I stood in front of him, blocking him. He had that look again. The one that told me he was done talking.

Except, he hadn't begun.

I'd dealt with that side of him for as long as I'd known him, but things were different now. He wasn't only shutting out a friend, he was shutting out his girlfriend and as much as I didn't want to change him, I didn't want any barriers between us, either.

"Drew."

"Ells, come on. I have to go."

Everything about his stance, from the way his shoulders stiffened to the sudden lack of warmth in his eyes told me not to push him. But if he didn't snap out of it, the entire day would stop being about the band's farewell to pub gigs and become about Drew's change in mood.

I hooked my arms around his neck, making him look at me. "You don't *have* to tell me what you're thinking but… I'm with you, Drew. Completely, one hundred percent with you. So if I am worried about Jason it doesn't change how I feel about you. I need you to understand."

His eyes softened a little. "I do understand, Ells. But that nagging voice in my head telling me I'm second best… I can't just turn it off. I can't tell you I'm not worried there'll always be a small part of you that would rather be with him."

"And that's okay." I ran my hands through his hair, curling the ends around my fingers. "Because every day, I'm going to prove you wrong."

Drew smiled, some of the worry melting away from his face. He kissed me softly. "I'll work through this, Ellie. I promise."

"I know you will. But right now, you have a rehearsal to get to."

With a sigh, he reached over to pick up the pieces of paper he'd been studying when I arrived. "What's that?"

Drew fanned the pages out in his fingers. "Song lyrics for the new album."

"Ooh, can I see them?" I reached out to grab them, but Drew was too quick.

"No," he answered, whipping them out of my grasp and opening the door. "You'll have to wait a while. We've still got a lot of work to do."

We stepped out into the corridor. "Fine. While you're working, maybe you could write a song about me."

His eyes, which a second ago were heavy with worry, flashed with mischief. "What makes you think I haven't already?"

Drew took advantage of my stunned silence to kiss me. I gently sucked his bottom lip, reinforcing exactly how much I wanted him. How much I wanted to do this with him forever. He let out another groan, forcing us to remember where we were. We both glanced up and down the hallway but, thankfully, there was nobody in sight.

"Yeah, I need to go right now." Drew straightened up. "I don't trust myself to stay any longer."

"Me neither."

The rest of my afternoon was spent on the phone to my mum, telling her my good news, then trying to work out how to pretend nothing had changed between Drew and me when we were around other people.

As it turned out, I didn't get enough time with Drew for pretending to be a problem. I was late to the pub and after I fought my way through to the backstage area, there were only a few minutes until they started their set.

"Ellie!" Mack threw his arms around me. "Drew told us you got the illustrator job. Congratulations!"

Joey patted my arm. "Proud of you, Ellie. Let me know when I can buy a copy of the book."

"Yeah, me too," Mack added.

A vision of two long-haired rockers intently reading a book about a lost bunny sent me into a fit of giggles. "I'll definitely let you know."

"Are you ready to go?" Jason leapt to his feet.

The guys confirmed they were indeed ready, but before they headed for the door, they all paused, exchanging understanding glances.

"This is it," Jason said. "Our last small gig."

Mack nodded. "I can't believe how much things are going to change."

"Or how much they've already changed," Joey pointed out. "We can't walk down the street without someone following us."

"And this is only the beginning. From now on, we'll be playing huge, sold out venues, and fighting women off with a stick."

"Speak for yourself!" Mack laughed. "I've got a woman, and I don't plan to swap her!"

"What about you, Drew?" Jason asked. "Are you ready for groupies sneaking into your dressing room?"

"We'll have security for that kind of thing." Drew's eyes narrowed. A strange bubble of tension surrounded them, and then burst as if nothing happened.

What the hell?

"I'd welcome any groupie who wanted to enter my room." Joey grinned.

Some colourful banter followed, but I blocked it out, wondering what was up with Drew and Jason. I shot Drew a questioning look, but he shook his head, as if to tell me it was nothing. Rubbish. It might only have been for a split second, but I saw it. I just didn't know what *it* was.

Razes Hell's last pub gig was exceptional. They played as if they'd never perform again, and the crowd was right behind them. It took forever for us to get out because so many fans wanted photos, autographs and the chance to speak with them. It was almost ten when we got back to the hotel and we wanted to eat before we went out again, so we rushed to the hotel dining room before it closed for the night. Surprisingly, it was still quite busy. Perhaps everyone had the same plan to eat late before hitting the town.

Dinner was the first chance we'd had to relax all evening but I still couldn't completely loosen up. I hadn't forgotten the weirdness from before the show. The tension hung in the air and I wondered if Mack and Joey were oblivious or ignoring it for the sake of keeping the peace. What made things worse was that I couldn't figure out what caused the frostiness between the brothers. They weren't fighting, yet their conversations were strained even though nothing obvious had happened to trigger the hostility.

"Should we all be sitting so close together?" I asked, trying to force myself to eat the spaghetti bolognese in front of me. My throat had closed up and I felt sure I'd puke if I swallowed another mouthful. "I mean, you're not supposed to be seen together off stage."

"It'll be fine, Ells," Drew said. "This place is packed. We have no choice but to share a table."

He gave my knee a reassuring squeeze which helped a little. I moved my foot closer to his in lieu of being able to hold his hand.

"This was a big night. You can't share that kind of moment and not feel a bit closer." Jason leaned across the table and reached for my hand. "Lighten up. We're supposed to be celebrating."

I forced a smile and pulled away before Drew's insecurities had a chance to spring up again. I could already feel his irritation levels rising.

"You know," Jason began, "we're lucky to still have Ellie in our lives. Most people would have run away screaming by now."

"Most people haven't known you as long as I have. Whatever happens, I'll always remember you when you were two little guys playing basketball in the back garden."

"That's how we met, right?"

"Yes. We played a lot of basketball that summer."

"And had lots of snowball fights in the winter."

"What's with the reminiscing?" Drew asked, his voice cold.

"I'm just thinking about how far we've come. We've been through a lot, the three of us. Not many people would stick with us the way Ellie has."

"Not true. Anyone who calls themselves a friend would stand by you through anything."

"Like when I was using drugs?"

"Yes. Like then."

Beside me, Drew stiffened, and another weird look passed between the brothers. "Ellie's pretty special that way."

The strain hit a peak as Jason's eyes narrowed and locked onto Drew's. "Is that why you've been sleeping together?"

chapter eight
The Girl Who Broke The Brooks Brothers

My stomach jolted and my gaze shifted from Drew to Jason, and back again. The boys didn't take their eyes off each other.

What just happened? One minute we were reminiscing about the old days, the next Jason spat out our secret as if he was talking about the weather. Mack and Joey stopped eating; Mack watching us closely, Joey staring at us open-mouthed.

"I knew it," Drew said. "You've been throwing out weird comments all night. You knew."

"I knew. I was waiting to see if you were ever going to tell me." He turned to me, anger dancing in his eyes. "Why didn't *you* tell me?"

"We didn't..."

"How did you find out?" Drew asked, cutting me off.

"I saw you kissing outside your hotel room."

Again, my stomach lurched. Whatever reasons we had for keeping him in the dark suddenly seemed insignificant. There wasn't only anger in his expression, but hurt too, and my insides twisted that we'd made him feel that way.

"Jason, I-"

"You don't need to explain." Drew took my trembling hand.

"Like hell you don't! You lied! Both of you lied to me!"

"Keep your voice down," Drew said sharply, as heads turned in our direction. The excited chatter in the room dulled to silence.

"Keep my voice down?" Jason repeated, not lowering his tone. "Why? Don't you want people to know you and Ellie have been screwing each other?"

The unmistakable sound of camera clicks punctured the quiet, and I felt my cheeks flame because there was nothing I could do to stop it. The words had been spoken, and countless YouTube videos of this moment would be all over the Internet within minutes. I didn't think even Derek would be able to stop this, and to be truthful, he probably wouldn't want to.

"Jason, please." My voice shook, panic taking hold. "Stop."

"Was it your idea not to tell me?" he demanded, fixing his glare on me.

I shook my head. "We're not doing this here."

"I want some answers!"

So did everyone in the restaurant, judging by the glee on their faces. What the hell kind of society did we live in that it was okay to film private, excruciating moments for the world to see? What happened to privacy? Decency? Or at least *pretending* not to listen when people caused a scene? Now, phones were held high in the air as if we'd agreed to air our problems in public; not a single one of them trying to hide what they were doing.

I stood up and Drew rose with me. "We'll talk later."

Jason got to his feet too and grabbed Drew's arm as we made to leave. "We'll talk now!"

The brothers stared at each other, locked in a silent mind game, and all I wanted was to get back to my room and put an end to this mortifying piece of performance art.

"Jason," I said. "Let's go somewhere and talk about this."

"We're not talking to him until he calms down." Drew shrugged free of Jason's grip.

"Don't walk away from me!"

Again, my eyes flicked between the brothers. Both of them silently begged me to do different things, their eyes willing me to choose. I wanted to go with Drew and leave Jason to cool off but we owed him an explanation. I was stuck in the one place I purposely never put myself because I couldn't, *wouldn't*, pick one over the other. Dating Drew didn't mean I would suddenly turn my back on Jason, but if I didn't, I knew exactly how Drew would react. Frustration rose inside me, followed by blinding panic because I knew neither of them would move until I made a choice.

"Ellie, come on," Drew said.

"Yeah, Ellie. Do as he says. Now you're with my brother, you don't get to make your own decisions anymore."

"What the hell is that supposed to mean?" Drew snarled, letting go of my hand and turning back to Jason.

"You're so used to trying to run people's lives, you can't see you're doing it! Ellie used to hate that about you. Your need to always be in control, but I guess things have changed."

The hurt on Drew's face made my temper flare, and since the other diners were already getting a show, I yelled, "Stop! Jason, the reason we didn't tell you is because up until a week ago there was nothing to tell. It's new, and if you'd asked instead of turning this into a fight, we could have explained. If you want to talk, we'll talk, but I'm not going to stay here and argue in front of a bunch of strangers!"

I turned and left the bar, heading for the sanctuary of my room. My legs wobbled with every step because my outburst had pretty much sealed my fate as an online sensation.

Jesus, why did Jason choose to blurt everything right out in the open? All he had to do was ask Drew privately, and none of us would have had to worry about being the next morning's headlines. Once inside my room, I kicked off my shoes and sat down on the edge of the bed, wondering if the guys were still fighting or if they'd separated, or gone elsewhere to talk. I probably shouldn't have left them together, but I couldn't stand to be the centre of attention any longer, and I certainly couldn't stand being stuck in the middle of their own personal feud.

A gentle knock on the door answered my question. I figured it was Drew. Jason would have knocked a hell of a lot harder.

The happiness Drew showed earlier was long gone, replaced with weariness. Forehead creased with worry, eyes filled with the stress of the last few weeks.

I pulled him inside and slipped my arms around his waist. "Are you okay?"

"You think I'm too controlling?"

He asked the question without returning my embrace and I stepped back. "What?"

"Jason said you hate how I always have to be in control. Is that what you think?"

Unbelievable. Jason announced to the world that we'd been sneaking around together, and instead of worrying about how it might impact all of us, the only thing he heard was his brother's anger-fuelled swipe at him.

I shook my head. "I can't believe you're asking me that."

"Why not? It's a simple question."

"It's a stupid question." I walked across the room to the window and stared out into the night. The view of traffic and excited revellers made me wish I was outside with them, hiding amongst them and making the most of the last of my anonymity before I became the girl who broke the Brooks brothers.

"It bothers me, Ells. That people see me that way. That *you* see me that way."

"I don't. I saw you that way when I was a child and didn't understand everything you had to do to keep your family together. But I grew up. *We* grew up."

"What are we gonna do now?"

Tearing my gaze away from the busy streets, I turned to him. "There's nothing we can do yet. We'll wait until he's calmed down and then we'll explain everything."

"This isn't going to be easy. It's not only about us, it's about me and him and... you and him." Drew heaved a sigh, raking his hands through his hair. "I didn't want this. I wanted us to be about us for a while. Before it became about Jason."

A small crack formed in my heart at his words. He looked defeated, as if Jason had won somehow. And he hadn't. Not even close.

"It hasn't become about him. I wish things hadn't happened the way they did, and I'm worried about how he took it. But us? We're still us."

Drew shook his head. "Being with you was always going to change everything. But I wanted to be with you, nobody else involved, for as long as possible. I guess I'm selfish and I don't want to share what we have yet."

A surge of warmth rushed through me. He wasn't so good at sharing his feelings, but when the words came out, he meant them.

I *felt* them.

I wound my arms around him, resting my head in that place on his chest where I could breathe him in.

"Nobody gets to share what we have. It's ours, Drew. Just ours."

Drew's heart beat a little faster when my fingers ran along the waistband of his jeans; his lips met mine before I could draw a breath. His kiss was always soft and intense, but there was so much more behind it this time. Like he was trying to throw aside his fears, and I was trying to prove he had nothing to be afraid of.

And something bigger. Something neither of us was ready to say out loud yet.

His hands, so gentle, bunched my shirt up at the sides until his fingertips lightly touched my skin, unmoving but full of intention.

This time, I wasn't embarrassed about the faint moan against his lips.

I reached for the bottom of his t-shirt, pushing it up, forcing us apart to tug it over his head, and we fell, side by side, onto the bed.

My breath hitched as my gaze travelled the length of his body. I'd never seen him this way before. I'd seen him shirtless, seen the look of hunger in his eyes, but never both at the same time.

My man.

I loved the broadness of his shoulders, and that he didn't waste time waxing his chest or sculpting his body into what was supposed to pass for the ideal way for a guy to look. *This* was how a guy should look. The flaming drum kit tattooed on his left bicep added to the appeal; his one moment of rebellion etched onto his skin forever.

"Ells?"

A flicker of self-consciousness showed but I wasn't about to stop staring. Couldn't. I hated that Lisa left him with the warped idea there was something wrong with him. Everything I saw was perfect.

"I think," I whispered as my lips trailed kisses across his cheek, tasting him from the top of his neck to the curve of his shoulder, "you're amazing." My fingers drifted down to his soft stomach, tracing patterns on his skin. When he smiled, I couldn't hold it in.

Didn't want to.

"I love you."

Drew's arm banded around me and he lifted me on top of him, shutting out all the space between us. The only sound was breathing; his heavy, mine shallow because he hadn't spoken. His eyes softened, lips parted a little, but still no words came out. A second passed.

Two.

Three.

The silence echoed in my ears.

Too soon.

Drew's mouth moved against mine, silently telling me it wasn't too soon. He pushed my hair out of my face, tucking it gently behind my ear.

"I love you, too."

My body collapsed against his. I'd never been the clingy girl who *needed* to hear "I love you." With Drew, I figured it would be a while. I didn't realise how much I needed to hear it from him until the words were spoken.

He laughed, softly. "You didn't think I'd leave you hanging, did you?"

"I thought you might because this is... it's all-"

Drew cut me off with another kiss. "It's fast. But it's right." A devilish grin formed as he tugged at the bottom of my shirt. "Can I take this off now?"

I nodded, and when his hands touched my back, my ability to speak disappeared. We shed our clothes with exploring, eager hands. Soft touches drifted across my curves; lips roamed freely over my skin causing whimpers of pleasure. I melted under his touch, moulding against him as if we'd been created to find each other so we could spend the rest of our lives doing this.

Drew started to roll me onto my back, but I tightened my legs around him, maintaining my position on top. His eyes flashed with uncertainty, silently asking if I wanted to stop.

"I like it up here." I gently traced my fingers across his chest again, then dipped my head for a kiss.

Relief replaced nervousness and he ran his hands down to my ass, kissing me harder, hand moving in between my legs. I gasped as he flicked a finger inside me and I pushed against it, wanting, *needing* more.

I didn't want to wait. I wanted to connect with him, to make every part of him mine.

"Ells, are you… do we need to…?"

His eyes glazed over as I slowly circled my tongue around his. "I'm on the Pill."

Least sexy sentence ever. If he'd been anyone else, I would have insisted on extra protection, but it was *Drew*. We knew each other's sexual history; we had nothing to worry about.

"Thank God," he breathed, running his hands down my sides. "I don't want to stop."

I closed my eyes, heart still hammering, readying myself to make him mine. To cross over the last line of friendship.

I was so ready.

Slowly, I lowered myself onto him, shivering as he slid inside for the first time.

"Ellie, look at me."

His voice was low and my eyes flickered open at his request. He watched me as I moved up and down on him, eyes unashamedly taking in every part. When his gaze met mine, it was as if he could see inside my mind, my heart; see everything I'd kept locked away for so long because it wasn't hidden anymore. It was me, showing him how much I wanted him, how much I needed to have him this close. And as he watched, I should have felt self-conscious. Exposed, and worried because maybe I wasn't at the most flattering angle, or maybe my thighs showed hideous cellulite. But Drew wasn't looking at any of that. His eyes were transfixed, as if my movements hypnotised him, tethering him to me.

My breath quickened, and I felt it building inside. The moment I knew would make me fall harder. Drew's hands tightened on my hips and I quickened the pace; faster, *faster*. His eyes locked onto mine, holding me in place. Hands slid up my back, bending me towards his chest. My already erect nipples stiffened as they brushed against him, and when he took one between his fingers, I couldn't stop from crying out. Sparks shot through me as he flicked and pulled, only gently, but enough to turn small shivers into trembles of pleasure.

I was close, *so* close. My legs weakened, breathing shallowed, and every sensation I felt seemed to merge together, building, climbing, until I burst, exploding into a million pieces. Stars danced in front of my eyes; wave after wave rolled and crashed. Within seconds, Drew bucked his hips, twitching beneath me, inside me, calling out my name as I collapsed down onto him, hot, overwhelmed. Exhilarated.

I buried my head into Drew's chest, listening to his pounding heart while trying to slow my own. Like an earthquake, I felt the aftershocks of the most intense orgasm I'd ever had sparking through my veins.

God, I love him so much.

Our skin was damp with sweat, but I snuggled in closer, not wanting to break the connection we'd built. Drew enveloped me in his arms and leaned forward to kiss the top of my head.

"I love you so much," he whispered, as if he'd heard my thoughts.

Aftershocks made way for butterflies and warmth, filling me from head to toe.

"I love you, too. So much."

I closed my eyes, losing myself in him, safe in the knowledge that no matter what happened in the morning, this night was ours.

Just ours.

chapter nine

The Very Definition Of Sex, Drugs
And Rock 'n' Roll

Don't open your eyes.

I heard the voice in my mind as I woke up, and for a moment, I took my own advice, afraid that when I allowed myself to re-enter the real world, the magic of the previous night would be snatched from me. I reached out, sure the only thing I'd touch would be empty space. *Wrong.* Drew was still sleeping beside me. I softly brushed my lips across his shoulder before resting my head against his chest.

It really happened.

I'd never let myself imagine how it would feel to sleep with Drew. Sure, my brain tried to take me there every time I watched him play a gig, or if he hugged me and his fingers lingered a bit too long on my waist. But I'd *needed* to block those thoughts out in order to look him in the eye without blushing. The real thing was better than anything I could have dreamt, and my pulse quickened at the memory.

Like everything with Drew, sex was intense. I'd never felt more connected to another person. That awkward, first-time-with-someone-new thing didn't exist between us. Instinct steered us in the right direction, drove us to know exactly what the other wanted, needed.

Once was *not* enough.

Drew's hand trailed down my back, and he mumbled, "Good morning."

The corners of my mouth turned up as I lifted my head for a kiss. He met my lips without hesitation and I sank into him, memories of the night before still strong at the front of my mind.

"Good morning." My voice came out in more of a sultry purr than I'd intended.

But damn, he looked good. The twinkle in his still sleepy eyes, and his slightly overgrown stubble. Flying high on the things we'd done together, plus the fact we were still naked, it was hard to keep control of anything, including my voice.

"Eleanor Jane," Drew said, smiling. "You sound like a porn star again."

"I'm okay with that."

From somewhere underneath my pillow, my phone rang. The intrusion was completely unwelcome, especially as I'd barely woken up yet. With an enormous sigh, I pulled it out.

Mum.

Parents call at the most inconvenient times.

If she called at this time of the morning, it usually meant bad news, and with a jolt of panic, I realised *I* was probably the bad news. The bad news in the papers. A post-sex glow, followed by the best night's sleep ever had helped dim the severity of Jason's dinner outburst, but it all came swarming back in a dizzying blur. With a shaking hand, I pressed the button to answer the call.

"Hi, Mum."

"Ellie, what the hell is going on? Do you know you're in the newspapers?"

Her frantic babbling did nothing to calm my nerves.

"I haven't seen them yet. But yes, I thought I might be."

"Why didn't you warn us? Your dad nearly choked to death on his porridge when he saw you! And Lucy says there are all kinds of rumours about you on the Internet!"

Trust my sister to investigate further. I couldn't blame her. I'd probably have done the same if the roles were reversed.

"Is it true?" Mum yelped. "Is any of it true?"

"Well, that depends on what you've read."

"Are you seeing Drew?"

I glanced at him. He'd turned onto his side, listening to my end of the conversation with an appropriate look of concern. I relaxed a little, butterflies fluttering inside me, beating out the fear of what the rest of the day would bring. Weird moment, being split between blissful happiness and stomach churning anxiety.

"Yes. I'm seeing Drew."

"For how long?"

"Around a week. I'm sorry I didn't tell you, but... we didn't tell anyone."

There was a lengthy pause. The kind that makes you wonder if you're about to get a huge telling off.

Please be cool with this, Mum.

"I'm happy for you. We all are. You should have told us sooner, though. Finding out this way wasn't fair."

Her words were heavy with disappointment. I snuggled into Drew, wishing we'd called our families last night. In hindsight, it was the obvious thing to do. In reality, we'd needed the last bit of time together without worrying about anyone but ourselves.

"I know. I really am sorry. Being with Drew is so new, *we're* still getting used to it. It was kind of... unexpected."

"Oh, Ellie." Mum laughed. "I've been waiting for this for a long time."

"What?" I screeched, making Drew jump. "What do you mean?"

It hadn't occurred to me anyone would ever have seen it coming. Jason certainly hadn't.

"Sweetheart, it's been obvious you have feelings for Drew for a while, and he adores you."

News to me. I mean, obviously, after he kissed me, I knew. Before, I'd spotted no signs of adoration at all. I hadn't searched for them because I was convinced they didn't exist, and it was far easier to live in a state of semi-denial than mope around after him, hoping he might notice me one day.

My silence seemed to make her forget her upset with me, and her tone softened. "Are you coming home today?"

"Yeah, we'll be back this afternoon."

"We want to see you. Both of you."

"Erm," I began, shifting my eyes to Drew again.

"We could order a Chinese tonight, and invite Michael and Jason too," Mum interrupted.

Ah. She'd pulled her classic Mum move, sensing me trying to wriggle out of it, and acting quickly to prevent me making up an excuse. I figured she wanted to see Drew and me together for herself. And, of course she'd want to invite Drew's dad and Jason to come along. Now we were more like one big family than ever.

Oh God. We hadn't had chance to talk to Jason yet. The last thing we needed was to be thrown into a room with him and our families before we'd cleared everything up with him. Why did everything have to be so complicated? Normal newly-formed couples get to spend their first few weeks together mapping out each other's erogenous zones, not explaining themselves to their relatives.

"Ellie, please. I'm sure you and Drew have a lot of... catching up to do, but this is a big thing for all of us. It would be lovely if we could get together tonight."

I winced at my mother picking up on one of the reasons for my reluctance. Completely unaware of what was being said on the phone, Drew slid his fingers down my spine, then around to my stomach. A shiver shot through me, my body still hypersensitive. The mischief on his face told me I was in trouble. My eyes widened, and he shrugged and mouthed, "I'm bored." I tried to conceal a giggle, as Mum said, "So, what do you think?"

Drew's mouth descended on my neck while I forced myself to concentrate on what my mum was saying. "Can we leave it until tomorrow? I don't know how the day is going to play out, but we've got a lot to sort out and we're really tired."

Drew nibbled at my shoulder, his hand closing over my breast, showing me we would never be too tired for *this*. I tried to wriggle away for the duration of the phone call but he wrapped his legs around me, trapping me between his thighs.

"Well, you don't have to stay for long."

I barely heard her. My limbs weakened as Drew's thumb rubbed across my nipple and I squeezed my eyes closed, hoping I'd get through the call without whimpering.

"Okay." My words came out far more breathily than anyone should ever sound while talking to their mother. "Dinner sounds good."

Drew grinned then dipped his head, taking my nipple in his mouth. My back arched as his tongue tormented me, flicking over the sensitive bud, his hands refusing to let an inch of my skin remain untouched. I bit my lip, holding in a moan.

"What time will you be there?" Mum asked.

Any freaking second!

"Erm, can I... ring you back later? I... I have to go."

As I ended the call, Drew gave an evil laugh, trailing kisses down my stomach. "Something wrong, Ells?"

I raked my fingers through his hair, pressing against him. "You're so going to pay for this later."

"Looking forward to it."

He grinned again, and I pulled him up to me to kiss him when a banging knock split the silence. Our bubble of horniness burst with a nearly audible pop and we both froze, eyes wide.

"What should we do?" I asked, carefully untangling myself from Drew to sit up. My head spun from the speed I was ripped from bliss to reality.

It had to be Jason. Drew sat up too, blinking a few times. "I guess we should answer."

"But he'll know you stayed the night and we-"

"Ellie, calm down. We've got nothing to feel guilty about."

Right. I was an adult, and yes, I was allowed to have sex with my boyfriend. But it was about more than that. We had plenty to feel guilty about.

We scrambled into our clothes, neither of us speaking. From the loudness of his persistent knock, Jason obviously hadn't calmed down overnight. With an apprehensive glance at Drew, I took a deep breath and opened the door.

Jason leaned against the door frame, his clothes crumpled, and his multi-coloured hair tangled and ratty. When he spotted Drew over my shoulder, he straightened up. "Should have known you'd be here."

"Jason, have you been to bed?" I asked.

"I want to talk to you. But I don't want him here."

Although his voice sounded calm, there was an edge that made me uncomfortable. Drew protectively wrapped his arm around me from behind. My body, still half asleep and desperate to be alone with him again, shivered at his touch and I gave myself a swift inward reminder now was *not* the time. I didn't need to look at Drew to know his eyes were fixed on Jason, defensive and prepared for a fight.

We never should have left him. We should have aired all this right away instead of letting him get worked up.

The joys of hindsight.

"I'm not going anywhere," Drew told him.

"Ellie."

I'd never been able to ignore Jason's pleading look. It wasn't fair to pull that trick out of the bag. Not now. He hadn't used it in years, hadn't needed to. It was reserved for when he'd really messed up and I was about to lose my last shred of patience with him. This was different. It was a test, and I wasn't interested in playing his game.

"Jason, please. Don't."

"Don't what? I want to talk. To you."

"I'm not leaving Ellie alone with you while you're angry," Drew said. "You can come in and talk to both of us or you can leave. It's up to you."

Jason switched his gaze from me to Drew. "She doesn't need you to speak for her."

"Stop!" I held up my hands, hoping to defuse their argument before it started. "It's too early for this. Jason, go get a coffee and give us chance to wake up. We'll meet you in an hour, and-"

"No." Jason's jaw set. "I want to do this now, and he needs to go. Or I can talk to the reporters downstairs who can't wait to find out exactly what happened here last night."

Jason's threat didn't bother me as much as the question of what people were reading about me while they ate their morning toast. He wouldn't follow through, anyway. I hadn't pressed the issue with my mum, but I had to find out how much damage had been done at some point. Better to hear the blunt truth now than walk around oblivious.

"What *exactly* do the papers say?"

"What do you think? There's a full transcript of everything that happened in one of the tabloids, and they all believe you're a whore who fucked me and Drew, and caused the fight on New Year's Eve!"

My legs weakened and I leaned against Drew for support. I'd expected it, of course. It was the obvious conclusion to jump to, but the reality of being spoken about that way was still a shock.

"None of this would be happening if you'd come to us yesterday instead of having a tantrum in front of everyone," Drew said.

"None of this would be happening if you two hadn't lied!"

As Jason's voice got louder, I half expected someone to poke their head out of their room to tell him to keep it down. Nobody came. All around us, people slept, while I stood between the two men I loved more than anyone in the world, knowing I had to make a choice. I couldn't walk away and deal with it later. *This* was later.

I heaved a sigh. "Jason, wait there."

I closed the door, and taking Drew's wrist, pulled him farther into my room.

"You're going to ask me to leave."

Drew's shoulders sagged, ripping another enormous hole in our cocoon of happy, because I *knew* the expression on his face. Resignation. The whole "second best" thing. It sort of stung that he still thought he fell behind Jason on my list of important people. A confession of love, and many hours wrapped up in each other obviously wasn't enough to make him understand. I always knew it would take time, but surely we'd made some progress?

"That's not what I was going to say." I took his hands. "But we're going to have a million questions thrown at us when we leave this hotel, and if we can calm Jason down, it's going to be a hell of a lot easier to tackle them. We need him on our side, Drew. Regardless of what the rest of the world thinks is happening in the band, we need him to be okay with this."

And I need you and Jason to be okay with each other again. Jason and I would be fine. We'd fight, we'd talk, and everything would be back to normal. It wasn't so easy between brothers. Common sense reminded me I'd be waiting a while for them to resolve their issues, but at least for now, we had to get on the same page.

Drew stared at my hands, gently stroking my palms with his thumbs. "You're shaking, Ells."

"Yeah. This is pretty much everything I didn't want."

"I know. I hate that he did this."

"We're not innocent, Drew. We should have told him."

"But we-"

"I know the reasons. But this is... it's a mess. We made a mess."

"I don't want to leave you alone with him." I opened my mouth to respond, and he added, "I trust you, Ells. But I don't trust *him* when he's so pissed off."

Wrapping his arms around my waist, I said, "I can handle him."

I waited while he weighed it up in his head. Clearing the air versus me being alone with Jason. Eventually, he said, "Do you promise to call me if he gets out of line?"

I meant to answer right away. Instead, I took a minute to cement the memory of how ridiculously sexy he looked first thing in the morning.

Another shiver.

No, Ellie. You don't have time to drag him back to bed. Yet.

The first day people found out about our relationship was supposed to be different. Full of relief, with Drew and I celebrating by holding hands in public, and having guilt-free sex, not avoiding contact with the outside world.

"Ellie?"

"I promise."

He leaned down to kiss me, his lips lingering on mine a touch longer than I could cope with. "Okay. Let's do this."

I was half tempted to wait until Drew was outside, close the door on both of them and hide until they sorted their differences out for themselves. When Drew turned the doorknob though, the hostility between the guys made it clear that wasn't an option. Without a word, Drew left, and headed down the corridor to his room. Drawing in a deep breath, I turned my attention to Jason. "Come in."

He stepped inside, not a trace of smugness on his face about getting his way. "What the hell's going on, Ellie?"

Well, there's nothing like getting straight to the point. But if that's the way he wants to play it.

"I'm in love with your brother."

Jason choked out a bitter, hollow laugh. "In love? With Drew? Come on, Ellie, be serious."

"I am being serious. I'm in love with him."

"No." He shook his head. "If you're screwing around with Drew, that's your choice, but don't try to tell me you two are in love."

"Since when have I ever screwed around?"

He paused to ponder my question, his eyebrows knitting as if I'd asked him to figure out a tough maths problem. In this case, one and one most definitely equalled two.

"How long has this been going on?"

"About a week," I replied, sinking onto the bed. The duvet was a crumpled mess from scrambling to get out from underneath it. I longed to throw it over myself, to block out the already awkward conversation with Jason, and hide until the gossip died out.

"Oh please!" Jason spat, pacing the floor. "It doesn't work that way. You don't just decide to fall in love with someone and you, Ellie, you don't fall for people so quickly, especially not people you've known your whole life. Not someone like Drew!"

Not someone like Drew. The words echoed in my head, infuriating me. I missed the days when Jason thought his big brother was cool, someone to look up to, instead of... whatever he saw now. Years had passed since then, and the saddest part was, the more respect Jason had lost for Drew, the more respect I gained for him. I got closer, was allowed a little bit further into Drew's mind with every one of Jason's screw-ups, and I learned how much more there was to him than the nag Jason always said he'd turned into.

Being with "someone like Drew" made me proud.

"It might not make sense to you. You've been too busy promoting lies, getting drunk, and shagging anything that moves! In the real world, where the rest of us live, Drew and I make perfect sense."

Jason flinched as if he'd been slapped. "You lied to me, Ellie." The first glimpse of hurt shone through his rage and my stomach clenched. "Do you think the lies weren't hard on us? I didn't enjoy keeping it from you, but we weren't ready to tell yet. It all happened so fast, and-"

"You didn't think I had a right to know about it straight away?"

"No more than anyone else."

There were certain - albeit rare - times when the similarities between the brothers were astonishing. Jason's face hardened, his eyes shut down.

"When did I stop being important?" he asked, and my insides twisted again, tying themselves into a knot of guilt.

"You didn't. We-"

"No. When did *I* stop being important? It used to be me. You used to love me. I loved you too, Ellie. Even if I wasn't good at showing it."

His words were unfair. Bringing up long dead feelings to make me feel worse than I already did. I didn't doubt he loved me. Well, as much as he was capable of when he'd just escaped small town life and discovered the very definition of sex, drugs, and rock 'n' roll. But it wasn't the same with him. It wasn't the same as the way I felt for Drew, or the other boyfriends I'd had. We were best friends who might have fallen in mad, crazy love if our circumstances had been different. And if the circumstances *had* been different, maybe our chemistry would have been different, too.

Put simply, we were never supposed to be together.

"It was a long time ago. We both know those feelings ended way before I finished uni."

"But I still mattered!" Jason shrugged out of his jacket, throwing it down to punctuate his words. As he did so, something flew across the room and landed right at my feet.

Time slowed as I watched the package on its journey.

I reached down to retrieve the item, Jason shouted at me to stop, and when my eyes connected with the mystery object my heart shuddered to a halt.

No. Please, no.

White powder, wrapped in cling film.

chapter ten
A Weird Symbol Of Your Willpower

The colour drained from Jason's face. "Ellie, it's not... it's nothing, really. Let me explain."

For a second, everything went fuzzy, and I was transported back. Back to *that* day.

I went into Drew's flat, closing the unlocked door behind me, and headed for the living room expecting to see Jason zoned out in the chair he'd barely moved from in two days. He'd been clean for eight days, only because he'd been forced to stay with Drew so he wouldn't be on his own for too long during the worst part of the withdrawal. For the first few days, Jason was restless and angry to the point of violence. He made his feelings clear when he kicked and shattered Drew's 42-inch television screen, then attempted to smash a window with the remote. But as time wore on, he'd become quieter. His sleeping patterns were messed up, and without cocaine in his system to keep him wired, he'd grown lethargic.

He wasn't in the chair.

Jason sat on the floor, shaking as he struggled to make neat lines out of the white powder in front of him.

My stomach lurched. His hair was lank, greasy, and he looked as though he'd been wearing the same clothes for days. What happened to the Jason Brooks I used to know? The one who always had a smile on his face. Always eager to book the next gig, always wanting to rehearse and write new songs. He'd gone. He'd been gone for a while, but I was done mourning the loss of the boy I'd worshipped during my teen years. Instead, rage ripped through me.

"Where did you get that?"

He jumped at the sound of my voice, his hand slipping, and knocking some of his charlie onto Drew's carpet.

"Ellie," he stammered. "I… It's not-"

The little colour left in his cheeks drained away, highlighting the darkness under his eyes. He clumsily got to his feet.

"Where did you get it?"

"I... I... It…"

"Have you used any of it yet?"

He shook his head, but his eyes flashed with the hunger to score.

"Get rid of it. You get rid of it now, and I won't tell Drew."

Not to save your ass, but because I cannot stand the idea of putting him through any more of your crap.

Watching Jason's downhill spiral had left both Drew and me helpless. No amount of interventions or trying to show him what would happen if he kept using made him understand how much damage he was doing to himself. Drew made me promise not to tell their father how much trouble he was in, but during the last few months, it had become impossible to hide. Still, it all fell on Drew to clean up the mess; not because their dad didn't want to help, but because Drew wanted to protect him from dealing with Jason while he was at his worst. He hurt in ways I couldn't fix with kind words, and my patience with Jason ran out a little more every time I heard Drew's heart breaking during our – now regular – evening phone calls.

"I need it, Ellie."

He looked down at his fingers, his hand twitching to get even the smallest speck of powder inside him. The tiny white particles clung to his fingertips.

"It's been eight days, Jason. Don't ruin it. Please."

He took in a ragged breath. "You need to leave."

"I'm not going anywhere until you've cleaned that up."

"I mean it, Ellie."

His tone darkened. A smart person would have run away screaming. I knew first-hand how strong Jason was when he was desperate for a hit; I still had the bruises on my arms from the last time, but I refused to let him snort another line.

"I'm not messing around here. I will vacuum that shit up if you don't. We're not going through this again."

He turned away as if he hadn't heard me. Before he could get back on his knees, I grabbed at his musty-smelling t-shirt and yanked him towards me, causing him to stumble. He crashed into me, the base of my spine colliding hard with the dining table. I let out a yelp of agony while Jason twisted around, pinning me in place. The pungent smell of his breath on my face made me flinch. "I told you to get out!"

I didn't want to be scared.

He's my best friend, I don't need to be scared.

But his face contorted with anger, and he pressed me harder into the table, his hands digging into my hips so hard I felt new bruises forming beneath them.

"When are you going to understand? You can't help me! This is who I am, okay? So, you and Drew, and everyone else who thinks you can fix me – just fucking stop!"

The physical pain I felt began to fade as a fresh wave of fury pumped through my veins. My whole body trembled, but I gathered my strength and screamed, "This is not who you are!"

"How the hell would you know? You haven't been around for months!"

"I was right here! I was here, but you pushed me away! You kept pushing, and I still kept coming back!"

"Well nobody asked you to!" He loosened his grip on me, but not before shoving me into the table once more. Another jolt of pain ripped through my spine but I refused to crumble.

"You know what you are?" Jason kicked the side of the sofa with his bare foot. "You're a goody-goody. You and Drew. You're both the same. Always trying to fix things. Always trying to turn people into something they're not. This is me, Ellie! I take drugs. I like drugs. They're better than people. People make me feel like shit! You make me feel like shit!"

Tears pricked my eyes then spilled over. I never treated him badly, not once. I kept treating him the same way as always, pretending nothing was wrong in the hope that somewhere inside him, the real Jason was still alive.

And it meant nothing to him. I meant nothing.

Angrily brushing away my tears, I straightened up. He wasn't looking at me anymore. Instead, he repeatedly kicked at the sofa, and I strode past him to sit down on the floor, right where I'd found him. He grabbed my hair but before he could pull, I smacked his hand away.

"Ellie, I swear to God, if you touch that, I'll kill you."

I didn't doubt his threat, but I was too angry to care.

"I want some."

The words flew out of my mouth easily. I wanted to know what was so damn good about cocaine that Jason couldn't, wouldn't give it up. I had to know.

I reached out to straighten up the cocaine lines, but he yanked me to my feet.

"What the hell is wrong with you?"

"Is it the money?" I shoved my hand into my jeans pocket and closed my fingers around a twenty pound note. "I'll pay."

Jason gripped my shoulders tightly. "Stop it," he snarled. "Stop it!"

"You always tell me how good it feels to score, so let me find out for myself. Come on, Jason. Show me what to do!"

He stared at me, his eyes burning with hatred. "Don't joke about that."

"Do I look as if I'm fucking joking? Let me have some."

"No!"

As he spat the word out, his fist connected with my cheek, knocking me to the floor. I curled up into a ball as the shock of his blow and the ache in my back overtook me. My limbs felt heavy, weak, lifeless.

"Ellie."

Jason sank to his knees, his hands resting on my shoulders but all I could feel was the crippling agony from everything he'd done to me, like razors, piercing at my skin.

Piercing at my heart.

"Ellie, I'm so sorry. Please, tell me you're okay. Please."

An ear-splitting shriek ripped from my throat, followed by heavy, body-quivering sobs, and I fell onto my side, clutching my knees to my chest as if it would keep me safe from the pain.

It couldn't. Nothing could.

Jason shuffled closer, leaning over me, and a hot tear that wasn't my own landed on my cheek. I didn't want to feel his guilt, or his regret. I didn't want to forgive him for hitting me, or for the things he said. His tears rained down on me, but I didn't move.

Time passed. Maybe seconds, maybe minutes. Probably not hours. From my position on the floor, I felt Jason suddenly grow tense.

"What the hell?"

I closed my eyes and covered my ears. Drew was going to kill him.

Snippets of yelling drifted around me until Drew softly spoke my name. He took my hands, exposing my throbbing cheek, and helped me to the sofa.

"Look at me, Ells."

I gritted my teeth, trying to hold myself together. "I can't."

"Please."

After a moment, I turned towards him. He knelt beside me, his eyes lingering on the mark where Jason's fist struck me.

"I'm so sorry. I should never have left him."

With a single shake of my head, I said, "Not your fault."

"It is my fault. I shouldn't have trusted him to stay here, but I had to go to Dad's and-"

"Stop. Stop blaming yourself for his screw ups."

My back twinged, making me jump. My back. From when Jason pushed me into the table. Where he screamed at me. Told me I made him feel like shit.

Drew bundled me into his arms, holding me tightly and I wept into his shoulder until there were no tears left. My head ached. Everything ached. I wanted a long, hot bath but the idea of going home and telling my family what happened made me feel sick. I couldn't face their questions yet.

"Can I stay here?" I reluctantly peeled myself away from him so I could wipe my eyes. "I want to stay here. With you."

"Yeah. Of course you can."

"Thanks."

"Ellie," he began, then paused and shook his head.

"What?"

"Jason said... He said he hit you because you were going to snort his coke."

I nodded. "I was so angry, Drew, I couldn't think clearly. He wouldn't let *me get near."*

"Did you hear what he said to me?"

"No."

Drew pushed my hair from my face, and touched my non-bruised cheek. "He said he had to stop you because he didn't want you to go through what he's going through. That he would never, ever let you be as stupid as he is. But I don't think he realised it until after he hit you."

"I know he's sorry. I do. I just don't care right now."

My heart ripped apart in my chest because I'd never imagined a time when I wouldn't want Jason around. He was as much a part of my life as my own family. But he'd hurt me in ways I never thought he was capable of and I didn't want to hear his apologies. Didn't want him near me.

Jason reached for my arm, but I snatched up the wrap of cocaine as I came out of my trance, and clambered over the bed away from him.

"Ellie, come on," he said, the lightness of his voice unable to disguise the panic in his eyes.

"You lecture me on keeping secrets, and you're carrying *this* in your pocket?" My hands shook because I didn't want to be holding cocaine, but I sure as hell wasn't going to give it back to him.

A second ago, he had screamed at me for lying about me and Drew, now I was quivering and clutching around sixty pounds worth of Class A drugs. "What is *wrong* with you? How could you-?"

"I'm not using, Ellie. Please sit down and listen."

I needed to be on my feet so I could pace, but the only way I'd know for sure if he was lying was by looking intently at his face, staring hard to find the truth. Reluctantly, I sat cross-legged on the bed, and Jason perched on the edge, sensible enough not to get too close.

"This isn't as bad as it looks. The coke was offered to me at the club last night. I told the bloke no, but he practically had it lined up for me. Said it was a freebie for a rock star, and I should stay in touch if I wanted some more. I didn't use any of it, I swear. I left the club straight away and came back here." He wiped his palms on his jeans, his body rocking back and forth.

Right there. The problem with fame. Until Drew's television appearance, when he unleashed all of Jason's secrets, nobody knew of his drug addiction. Stories about celebrities being given freebies weren't exactly unusual, but Jason's past made him way too easy a target for dealers.

"Why did you keep it?" I asked, not letting my focus waver from him. "Why didn't you flush it?"

He closed his eyes. "I wanted it. I wanted it bad. I never had any intention of snorting a single line, but when I tried to get rid of it... I couldn't."

I glared at him. "Dammit, Jason! After all this time? After all you went through to get off it? This is so bloody typical of you. The spotlight leaves you for five minutes, and you do this!"

"Do you seriously think I planned for you to see this? Jesus, you sound like Drew already! He thinks I'm a narcissistic prick but I'm not, and I'm not an idiot. The last thing I need is you on my case about cocaine I wasn't going to use!"

"So you weren't planning to use it, just keep it forever as a weird symbol of your willpower?"

"I don't know!" Jason threw himself backwards on the bed, his head landing close enough to my feet that I could kick some sense into him – if I were a violent person. I'd already hurt him, suggesting he did this for attention. It *was* a Drew-like thing to say, but in the moment, I'd been unable to censor my words before they flew out. Jason didn't need to seek out attention, it naturally found him, and he would never have been stupid enough to plant drugs on himself as a way to point the spotlight back to him. He wasn't *that* desperate for publicity.

"You have to throw it away. Now."

"I know. I know."

I watched as he breathed deeply, his hair splayed all around him, and angry as I was that he'd crossed a dangerous line, I felt his despair. He wasn't lying when he told me he wasn't going to use, or at least, he didn't intend to. But the lure of cocaine still had a grip on him, even after two years clean.

"I'll never go back down that road again, Ellie. But... I need you to help me right now."

"What can I do?"

"Don't tell anyone. Especially not Drew."

"Oh, come on. You can't ask me to-"

"Ellie, please." Jason sat up, pulling his legs onto the bed. "He can't find out about this."

I would have been slightly less concerned about lying to Drew if we were still just friends. Or maybe not. Since our relationship *had* changed, the not getting in the middle thing was much harder.

Bloody hell.

Drew is already struggling with everything Jason did before. If he finds out Jason has drugs right now, he'll never forgive him. If we get rid of the cocaine immediately, it'll be done.

Except, you'll have lied.

"Don't," I stood up. "Don't give me the beggy eyes. We just argued about how messed up everything gets because of lies, and now you want me to do it again?"

I squeezed the wrap of cocaine between my fingers, hoping I could make it vanish along with every other nightmare that had happened since I woke up.

"Please," Jason said.

"I believe you didn't intend to use this. But now the temptation is back-"

"It never goes away, Ellie. It's better. Easier every day. But it never goes away. On the rough days, there's still a voice in my head telling me I can make all my problems go away with a quick fix. Last night was the worst I've felt in a long time, and that dealer put the solution right in my hands." Again, he paused to wipe his sweaty palms on his jeans. "I could feel it. The buzz. I knew how good it would feel to take the hit and forget everything, and I hated myself for it. For being so fucking weak, because you're right, Ellie. It's been two years. It should be over."

I used to know this. When Jason first spiralled out of control, I learned everything I could about cocaine addiction. I spent hours trawling the Internet to soak up every bit of information. I knew the risks, the withdrawal process, I learned about triggers, and I understood there wasn't an end. I sobbed while reading some of the most heart-breaking stories, not knowing if one day Jason would end up the same way. Another sad story, leaving behind a grieving family and friends to ask themselves what they could have done to change the ending.

Time had healed the physical wounds Jason inflicted on me, but locked away in a corner of my mind, I remembered every detail. Sometimes I could still hear the smack of his hand hitting my face, and feel the agonising realisation that everything I did, all the time I'd spent learning ways to help him were for nothing because I *couldn't* help. Not then.

"You couldn't flush it," I said, my voice trembling. "That's the part I'm worried about."

He turned to look me in the eye. "If ever there was a time I needed it, last night was it. The morning after, the coke's still all wrapped up. Doesn't that count for something?" Jason stood in front of me, his hands on my shoulders. "I'm so sorry. I've messed everything up, but I've never needed your help more. Please, help me get rid of this and don't tell Drew. Please."

Help me.

I nodded, tears filling my eyes as I sent up a silent prayer I was doing the right thing. "Okay. Okay."

Relief made him fling his arms around me. I shrugged him off and went to the bathroom, unwrapping Jason's stash and shaking it off the cling film and into the toilet. When every speck had gone, I stuffed the wrapper inside an empty shampoo bottle in the bin and went to the sink to wash my hands. The hot water burned my skin as I scrubbed all traces of the drugs away. Therapeutic. If only soap could wash away guilt.

You could tell him. Tell Drew, and the guilt will be gone.

My heart lurched as I thought of him because the situation wasn't that straightforward. Revealing the truth would only intensify the old resentment, put the band under strain they didn't need, and for what? A one-off. I'd known Jason long enough to spot a lie, and everything he said was true. I *felt* it.

"Jesus, Ellie, stop!"

Jason grabbed my waist, pulling me out of my thoughts and away from the sink, hands bright red from the violent scrubbing I'd subjected them to. I stared down at them, realising tears were streaming from my eyes.

"Here." He took a towel from the rail and gently dabbed my raw digits so as not to hurt them more.

There he is.

The Jason from the old days, who would rather throw himself in front of a bus than risk causing me pain. I didn't see this guy often anymore. Our friendship was solid enough to survive the changes he went through, but he could never go back to who he used to be. Too much had happened. These little glimpses of my first ever best friend reminded me he still lived deep inside the man who stood with me now.

"What can I do to make this okay?"

"You could tell Drew, and not make me do this. You could not put me in the position where I have to lie to him."

"Ellie-"

"I know. I know why you can't. But I don't... I don't want to be-"

"If I could do today again, I would. I don't want you in this position either. I'll do anything else for you, but I can't tell him."

I had to try. It didn't lessen my guilt any, and I knew what Jason's answer would be before I asked the question. The worst part was, I understood why he didn't want Drew to find out. It would tear them apart, rip another hole in their already damaged relationship. I couldn't see any other way to protect both of them besides keeping Jason's secret.

Even if it killed me to do it.

"All I need from you is a promise you'll never touch cocaine again. Not even if someone tries to force you."

He stopped drying my hands, and his fingers closed around mine. "I can do that."

He meant it. Maybe more than anything he'd ever said in his life. I only hoped it would be as easy to resist the temptation the next time someone presented him with a quick fix, because there *would* be a next time. That much I was sure of.

Jason wrapped his arms around me again, and I hugged him back.

"I'm sorry. For the way I acted last night. And for... for bringing up the stuff from the past."

Right. The stuff none of us ever spoke about.

"Why did you?"

"Because I *am* a narcissistic prick," Jason said, and I let out a small laugh. "This thing with you and Drew has nothing to do with me, or us, or anything that happened when we were younger. It's just... I always thought of you as mine. My Ellie. The girl who never gave up on me when you had so many reasons to walk away and never come back. You being with Drew scared me because I don't want to lose you. I don't want the way he thinks of me to affect the way you think of me." I pulled back from him a little, and he continued, "I'm not blind. I've seen how he's been around me the last few weeks. I know what this feud is doing to him. To both of us."

"Why didn't you say so? Why didn't you talk to him?"

"Because… you know how he is. He'll only hear when he's ready."

True story.

I should have given Jason more credit. It wasn't fair of me to assume he didn't notice the problems because he never complained. The small part of me that held onto the pain Jason caused allowed me to believe he was selfish and oblivious. When it came to Drew, I should have expected more from him.

"He's my brother, Ellie. I love him, but he's not the only one who's still angry."

With the weight of everything that had happened in the hour since I woke up, the extremes of emotion, I suddenly felt exhausted. Too exhausted for an in-depth conversation about how to patch up years of issues between the brothers, and way too tired to deal with gossip-hungry journalists.

"Can you make this mess over me and Drew go away? I'm not news, Jason. I'm an ordinary girl who fell in love with an extraordinary man, and I want to be with him in peace."

Jason took in a deep breath and blew it out slowly. His eyes softened and he nodded.

"I'm sorry. Give me an hour or two and I'll fix it. I promise."

chapter eleven
The Happy Lady

True to his word, Jason didn't waste any time calling Derek to implement some damage control. Razes Hell fans weren't the kind to be interested in tabloid gossip. For the most part, they were quite an emo crowd, but the readers of celebrity news found the whole "love triangle" aspect fascinating. I'd taken a quick peek at some of the more popular gossip websites on my iPad, and seeing grainy, unflattering shots of myself, and guesses about what really happened did nothing to cheer me up.

While I waited for Derek to arrive at the hotel, I called my mum back. If she had any idea what Drew was doing to me during our last call, she didn't mention it, thankfully. I reluctantly agreed to us having dinner with our families later, even though Drew and Jason weren't talking and it would be awkward as hell. Making arrangements took my mind off the news and Jason's near-dabble with drugs. I also received an email from Janet Black, asking me to take some time to carefully read the terms of the attached contract for the illustrating job. Not a problem. It would probably be a few days before I had the brain power to take it all in.

Derek arrived at the hotel in less than an hour, and when he got to my room, he was not his usual put-together self. What was left of his grey hair flapped on one side, and his shirt and trousers were unusually crumpled, as if he'd been attacked by an angry mob.

An angry mob of journalists.

"Okay, we need to sort this out fast," Derek said, trying to tidy his hair. "Those reporters want blood, and if I don't give them something, they're going to get pissed off."

"Wow, way to calm me down. So, what's the plan?"

Derek shrugged. "First you have to tell me what's happening."

"Didn't Jason explain?"

"He told me that you and Drew are together, and the rest I read in the paper."

"What else do you need?"

"I need to know what you want from this."

"I want this to go away!" I tried not to shriek at the only person who had a shot at helping. "I don't want to be the girl who might have caused the fake feud; I want to be the girl I was yesterday. The one I've always been, who stays in the background. Can you make that happen?"

Derek watched me thoughtfully. In fact, he stared so intently, I wondered if I had food in my teeth. "You're unusual, Ellie. You're an artist, and you've been given a huge platform to launch your career from. Are you sure you don't want it?"

"I'm sure. I've been asked to illustrate a children's book, and I got the job through my own hard work. I want to keep it that way. Fame is not my thing."

"Okay. But you need to understand what you're getting into here. Everyone's gone nuts for Razes Hell, and like it or not, if you're with Drew, you're going to get attention. I'm talking constant speculation, cameras in your face, strangers shouting crap at you in the street and the occasional death threat from jealous fans. Are you ready for it?"

If our relationship hadn't been forced into the open, nobody would care who I was. Thanks to the wonderful people who invented camera and video phones, that dream was dead. Derek was right, though. Even if we didn't court publicity, the bigger the band got, the more people would want to snoop inside our lives. It was so easy for outsiders to intrude, with social media giving hundreds of thousands of people a tip-off to someone's whereabouts in seconds.

But you have Drew. The beginning of a panic attack at the immense upturn my life was about to go through eased as I thought of him. He'd always kept me safe, even before we got together. Now, he was mine, so if we were forced to share a little bit of what we had with the world sometimes, it would be worth it. Being with him was worth it.

"There are plenty of wives and girlfriends of famous people who don't flaunt who they are. This has all started off in the worst way, and I don't want anyone to think I'm with Drew to promote my own career. So, yes. I'm ready to take whatever comes, but I will stay out of the spotlight as much as I can because it's not mine. It belongs to the band."

Again, Derek silently gazed at me, admiration growing in his eyes. "You're a good girl, Ellie."

"You say that as if you doubted me."

"I didn't. You've been with the guys through everything so I know you're not a hanger-on who wants to be associated with rock stars. But people with the best of intentions sometimes lose who they are when an opportunity comes along. Whether you see it or not, this *is* an opportunity for you." He paused, and blew out a breath. "If you want this to go away, I'll release an official statement this morning explaining there was a misunderstanding, and any in-band fighting had nothing to do with you. Your name's already out there, but I won't mention it again, and if reporters contact you, don't speak to them. Don't react if they follow you. Keep walking, pretend you can't see them. If you don't give them any gossip, they'll lose interest."

"That's it? That's all there is to it?"

"Yes. Journalists are like flocks of seagulls. If you feed them a tiny morsel of food, they'll keep on coming back for more. If you don't, they'll lurk, waiting, then move on when someone else throws them a crumb."

I smiled. "So. No crumbs for the reporters."

"Exactly. Now," Derek added, "I've arranged for a couple of cars to meet you at the back entrance. You can decide between yourselves who goes in which car, but you're not going back in the van. I talked to the band before I came in here, and they'll be ready to go when you are."

"Wait. You arranged for two cars to take us back to St. Ives?" Derek nodded. "You need to be safe, and the only way to ensure you are is to have you driven home in different vehicles."

"What about the band's equipment?"

"I'll drive the van home myself."

So, he does care. Not once had I ever seen anything from him but greed and a desire to push his way to the top through any means necessary.

"Thank you, Derek."

"No problem. I'm gonna sort this statement out now, so you should pack up and get out of here as soon as you can."

It didn't take long to throw my clothes, shoes and phone back in my bag, and head down the hall to Drew's room. Only a couple of hours had passed, but waking up beside him seemed a million years ago. I needed his arms around me, to feel connected to him again, and to lose myself in that place where everyone and everything else ceased to exist.

My plan was scuppered when I entered Drew's room and the whole band was in there. Not a hint of the camaraderie from the night before remained. The tension was so thick it was comparable to being smacked in the face with a cricket bat. Everyone's bags were strewn on the floor, and I threw mine on the heap. "What's going on?"

Mack's gaze flicked between Drew and Jason. "Everything's fine," he said. "We should probably be on our way soon."

"Good idea." Drew picked up our bags. "Ellie and I will share a car; you three can take the other one."

Drew started towards the door, not giving me a second to figure out why everyone was so tense.

"Wait," I said. "Jason, are you okay?"

Waves of irritation from Drew threatened to knock me to the floor. Leaving without checking on Jason was not an option, though.

Not after the morning's events.

"I'm fine. I'll call you later."

Silently, I asked him again, hoping he read the bigger question in my eyes. *Are you really okay? Do you need me?* ' He gave me a reassuring smile and a small shake of his head, easing my concern a little. Something still wasn't right, but I trusted he'd be fine with Mack and Joey.

"Okay. I guess we'll see you later."

The second Drew and I left the room, I grabbed his wrist, making him stop. "Hey. Do you want to tell me what happened in there?"

Drew shook his head. "It's not important."

"Not important? It was important enough to silence a room full of musicians who should be celebrating right now."

"Hard to celebrate when my brother screwed you over, and you don't seem to care that this mess is all his fault."

My heart sank, not because I didn't expect this, but because I'd hoped Drew would at least try to understand my position in all of the chaos. Did he expect me not to care how Jason felt after this gigantic bombshell was dropped on him?

"I care, but it's done now. He apologised, he got Derek to come here to sort it out. What more can he do?"

Drew stared at me, his expression cold enough to raise goose bumps across my skin. "It's really that easy for you, isn't it?"

It might not have been if I hadn't been distracted by the cocaine. Jason staying clean concerned me way more than his tantrum. Of course, I'd promised I wouldn't tell Drew, which seemed like a massive mistake the longer he fixed his icy glare on me. Keeping the peace between them – or at least not making things worse – depended on me not telling Jason's secret. No matter how much I hated the look on Drew's face.

"It has to be," I said. "I don't want to be eaten up with anger for the rest of my life about stuff I can't change."

"Like me, you mean?"

I shook my head. "Don't try to pull me into a fight. It's been a hell of a morning, and I'm not up for arguing."

"I'm not trying to argue, I'm trying to understand how you can be so okay with what he did!"

A door opened, and a young couple stepped out of their room, pausing to do a double take as they passed us. They stared, as if waiting for us to continue our argument, as if we were reality TV stars putting on a show for their enjoyment. To their credit, they didn't linger when we stayed silent, but I was done being in front of people. I grabbed Drew's arm and dragged him back into his room.

Jason, Mack and Joey were picking up their belongings ready to head home. They stopped as we entered, and I said, "Mack, Joey, could you give us a few minutes, please?"

The guys nodded, picking up their bags as Drew dropped ours back on the floor. Once they left, I took a deep breath. "We need to talk."

Drew and Jason refused to look at each other; I stood between them, heart racing. My body felt heavy, as if I'd emerged from a nightmare, only to find it was my reality. If the worst thing to happen that morning was me finding myself splashed all over the tabloids, I would have coped. But it was never just about me. It was about Drew and Jason too, and how our lives all tangled together like my grandma's bag of knitting yarn. She used to dump it out on the floor, prod around with the threads, then give up, deciding it was all too difficult before throwing it back in the bag. That's how we were. Strands, knotted together. Occasionally, one of us would tug in the hopes it would all unravel, but mostly, we stayed the same. Sometimes the knots got tighter. But the end result was always us stuffing it away so we didn't have to deal.

"This has to stop. It hurts me to watch you slowly destroying yourselves. Neither of you want to make the first move in sorting this out so I'm doing it for you. Whatever you want to say to each other, say it. Now. Start talking so you can fix this."

Jason shook his head, leaning back against the wall and Drew sat down on the bed with a look of defiance on his face, letting me know he had no intention of speaking first.

Jason wasn't kidding when he said Drew would only hear when he was ready.

"You can't fix us, Ellie," Jason said. "If you thought it would be easy, you'd have done this before now."

He was right. This was never going to be a one conversation thing. Plus, it wasn't my place to heal their rift, only to be there for them both while they worked it out for themselves. Unfortunately, it had become increasingly clear they were incapable, or unwilling, to do that.

"Please. Can't you try? You haven't spoken to each other without arguing since yesterday."

"We wouldn't have argued if Jason hadn't fucked everything up."

Jason's shoulders slumped, his hair hung limply around his shoulders. "Yeah, we just had this fight. I fuck things up, and he comes along and clears up all my mess. I know the story. I've been hearing it most of my life. I'm an ungrateful tosser who doesn't appreciate him."

As a friend, you are useless.

How could I have not seen Jason was in as much pain as Drew? He bounced back from everything without complaining but that didn't mean he didn't feel anything. Sometime between him finding out about me and Drew, and our earlier conversation, a door had been opened. A door which, in some ways, had been bolted tighter than Drew's.

"Is that what you think this is about?" Drew demanded. "You think I give a shit that you don't appreciate me? You never have, I don't expect you to start now."

Jason's head snapped up. "Why don't you tell me what it *is* about? Maybe then you can stop using Ellie as a way to prove how much better you are than me."

My heart stopped, and Drew jumped to his feet, grabbing Jason's shirt and shoving him hard against the wall. "You can say whatever you want about me, but don't ever suggest my feelings for Ellie aren't real."

I'd seen Drew angry a lot of times, but I'd never seen him move so fast, or lay a finger on anyone. It wasn't a side of him I wanted to see again.

With shaking hands, I tried to pull him away but his grip stayed firm. "Drew, stop."

"Did you hear what he said?"

"I heard him, but it's not... I don't think he-"

"I think what Ellie's trying to say," Jason interrupted, pushing Drew off, "is that I wasn't saying your feelings aren't real. But don't try and tell me you didn't get a kick out of rubbing it in my face."

Oh God. Why won't he let this drop?

"Jason, you never wanted me that way. Not for anything more serious than a few kisses when we were young and drunk."

"But you were my best friend."

"How has that changed?" I asked, looking right into his eyes. Again, we communicated in complete silence and I used our skill to remind him I'd helped him earlier. Slowly, some of the tension left his body. "I get that you're still here for me, but it'll be different. And that's why he's so fucking smug. He thinks he's won."

I couldn't tell him he was wrong. It was the truth. Not a truth that was as twisted as it sounded though. In Drew's eyes, being with me might have felt like a win, and not because I was arrogant enough to believe I was a worthy prize but because, for once, he let himself be vulnerable and it paid off.

"This isn't about me."

I stepped away from them, taking Drew's place on the bed. The tiredness I'd felt earlier washed over me again. This was too damn hard. Too much anger, too much suppressed agony. Too much hate between brothers who used to have nothing but love and respect for each other.

"Ellie's right." Jason said. "This is about us."

Drew turned away. "I don't want to talk about it."

"Maybe *I* want to talk about it! I'm sick of this passive aggressive bullshit, Drew. You wanna tell me how much you hate me? Do it! You wanna tell me how much you resent having to look after me my whole life? Come on, I'm right here. Just say it so we can move the fuck on."

"Talking isn't going to change anything."

"So we're going to carry on this way? Being pissed off with each other because you can't let go of the past?"

"The past that's been dragged up every day since you agreed to let Derek bring it out into the open?"

"We both agreed."

"If you knew me as well as you think you do, you'd know I hated the idea from the start. And I did tell you."

"You let it drop!" Jason pushed away from the wall, shaking his head again as he paced the room. "This is a waste of time. I appreciate you trying, Ellie, but I can't do this on my own."

Drew spun around to face Jason, eyes blazing. "What do you want from me?"

"I want you to stop acting as though I'm the reason for every bad thing that's happened to you! I've done some shitty things, but I've worked damn hard to make up for them. Do you have any idea how hard it was? How hard it still is?"

"Try being the one who had to hold everything together while you were *doing* shitty things! You can apologise as much as you want, but you can't take away the times I found Dad crying, blaming himself for what you did. Hearing him calling himself a bad father because he thought he didn't do enough for you after Mum died was one of the worst times I've ever been through! He thought everything you did was his fault!"

Michael Brooks was the picture of a typical, old-fashioned English gent. He stood up when a woman entered the room, held doors open, pulled out chairs so you could sit down at dinner, and completed the stereotype with a stiff upper lip. Watching him suffer was as heart-breaking as witnessing Jason's rapid decline.

Jason sagged back against the wall, the pain on his face, on both of their faces, made tears flood my eyes. Every harsh word they exchanged pierced through me like knives slashing at my soul, and I'd brought them to it. Forced them to slog it out, knowing how gut-wrenching it would be. I didn't want them to hurt anymore. *I* didn't want to hurt anymore. But whether the conversation happened or not, everyone hurt.

"I didn't know," Jason said, quietly.

"You didn't care! You didn't care about anyone but yourself, and that's never changed! You've always been selfish, and I'm done fixing everything you break!"

Without looking at either of us, Drew picked up our bags again, and walked out, slamming the door behind him.

I couldn't move yet. My body trembled, and when I glanced at Jason I saw he was shaking, too. For the second time in one day, I was torn in half. I wanted so much to be with Drew. To hold him, and tell him I was sorry for pushing him. Sorry for making him dig further into those painful memories when all it did was make everything worse. But how could I leave Jason?

"Go to him, Ellie." Jason lowered his head, and I was pretty sure his hair hid some tears.

"Jason, I-"

"He needs you more than I do."

"I don't think that's completely true," I told him, rising on wobbly legs. "I can't leave you like this."

I reached for his hand, and he sighed. "I've been waiting for him to say those things for a long time. I've expected it every day, and every day, he kept them bottled up." His voice cracked, making my own tears spill. "You need to go to him. Take care of him."

"Who'll take care of you?" I pulled at his hand to make him look at me.

He gave me a small smile, one that didn't quite reach his moist eyes. "I've got Mack and Joey waiting for me. I'll be okay with them. When I get home I might... I might talk to Dad about the things Drew said. And tomorrow, I'll call you. But right now, you have to go. Please."

One comment in a conversation so full of horrible memories brought Jason down. He'd heard some of it before, but both Michael and Drew shielded him from the extent of the heartbreak he caused. I'd never understood why. The first time I spoke to Jason after he hit me, I didn't hold back. We both wept, transporting ourselves back to that day, and even after, we knew it wasn't an instant fix for our friendship. It was one step towards getting back to where we were. Or as close as we could after such a huge break of trust. Maybe that was why he was so different with me. We cleared the air completely. I didn't use the possibility of a relapse as a reason to keep my feelings in. Perhaps it was selfish of me, but I wanted my friend back. Without total honesty, I couldn't see any other way to make it happen.

I nodded. "Okay." I put my hand up to his cheek, and wiped away a tear with my thumb before heading outside to find Drew.

I ran along the corridor and took the stairs down to the lobby where Mack and Joey stood close to the reception desk, away from the pointed camera lenses waiting to snap them.

"Have you seen Drew?"

"He went out the back exit." Mack's eyebrows furrowed with concern. "What happened?"

"Long story. Can one of you go up and check on Jason? I'm sure he'll fill you in. How do I get out of here?"

"Go back the way you came, and at the bottom of the stairs, there's a fire door. That's where the cars are waiting."

"And there are no reporters out there?"

Joey shook his head. "It's as if they've never stalked anyone before."

I let out a small laugh. "Thanks, I'd better go. Please look after Jason for me and... make sure he gets home safely."

The guys nodded, and I knew I could trust them to keep Jason from falling apart any further. With a quick smile, I dashed out the way Mack instructed, and almost tripped over Drew as I opened the fire door. Two cars waited for us, but he hadn't made it that far.

He sat on the step, hunched over, shivering from the cold.

A full-sized version of how he sat the first day I met him.

Without a word, I sat beside him, and wrapped my arms around him. His head hit my shoulder, and he let out a sob, puncturing the silence of the back street, and simultaneously puncturing another hole in my heart as his tears seeped into my shirt. I held him tighter, my own tears falling hard.

I'd never seen him cry before. Not when he broke his arm after falling off his bike. Not when the postman delivered a letter addressed to his mother two years after she died. Not when Jason was carted away to rehab, merely a shadow of who he used to be.

"I didn't mean to... I... Ellie-"

"Shh. It's okay."

He tried to speak again, but nothing came out. Nothing more than a croaky sound before he took a shuddering breath, then gave up. I kissed the top of his head, waiting for his long pent-up emotions to ease a little. When he was ready, he looked up and wiped his eyes, exhausted. "I couldn't stop myself." His eyes stared straight ahead and I knew he wasn't completely with me. Lost in thought.

So I waited.

"He's my brother, Ells. It's not okay that I hate him and love him, and I'm angry with him, and I feel bad for him. Right now I want to punch him in the face for the things he said to me, but I also want to be his big brother, and protect him from what *I* said to him. I don't know which instinct is strongest."

I ran my hand soothingly across his back. "Which instinct is always strongest in you, Drew?"

"The one that wants to punch him in the face."

I laughed softly. "No. It's not. Recently, maybe. But mostly, it's always been the big brother thing."

"I wanted to hurt him, Ellie. All I did was remind myself of the painful crap we went through. The stuff I try not to think about. And the worst part is I'm not finished. Not even close." He hung his head again. "Do you remember my mum?"

"Not very well," I answered, sifting through recollections in my mind. "I remember a lady used to live in your house, and sometimes I saw her playing in the garden with you and Jason. She was always smiling. She was the happy lady who used to live next door."

"Yeah. That was Mum. The happy lady." Drew looked up at me. "When she got ill, sometimes I'd go to her room and sit with her. Even when she was almost gone, she kept smiling. She used to tell me to look after Dad and Jason. She said if she had to leave us, she knew we'd be okay because she could count on me to take care of everything. I don't think she meant to put such a huge burden on me. She wasn't telling me to give up my own life for Dad and Jason, but I was young. I thought the least I could do for her was look after our family. Keep Dad from falling apart, and keep Jason out of trouble. I did okay with Dad. But every time Jason did something bad, I felt like I'd let my mum down. When he got worse, when he was using drugs and stealing from us to get his next fix, I blamed myself. I thought, *If Mum was here, he wouldn't do this, she'd be able to stop him.'* I couldn't. I couldn't keep my promise to her." He paused then turned away as he broke down again. "I just wanted her back, Ells. I wanted her here to tell me what to do."

Without ever meeting her, I wanted her back too. I wished she could see what an exceptional person she'd brought into the world. A little boy who only wanted to fulfil his mother's dying wish, who grew into a man who loved his family so much, he tore himself apart for feeling the way anyone in his position would have felt.

"Drew. You didn't fail."

"I failed Jason by not being his brother."

"That's not true. Yes, you were overprotective a lot of times, but you never stopped being a brother. You were there for him, even when he didn't deserve it."

"I'm fucked up, Ellie. Losing Mum messed me up. I should have dealt with it better. Sooner. Do you know what Lisa said to me when she left, Ells? She said she'd never marry someone like me, and I'd never be good for anyone because I didn't have a female role model when I was growing up, which meant I had no way to know how to treat a woman."

Five years. Lisa was with him for five years, and those were the last words she spoke to him? The man who loved her so much he'd have walked through fire for her. What kind of person uses the death of their boyfriend's mother as a way to explain why she's leaving him?

"Is she right?" he asked.

I took his face in my hands. "Listen to me. You never treated her badly. Not once, Drew. You were everything a boyfriend should be because you learned all you needed to about relationships from seeing your parents together. You told me."

"Did I?"

"Yes. It wasn't too long after we met. I asked if you remembered your mum. You told me the thing you remembered the most was how your mum and dad always held hands when they watched TV together, and they never left for work without a goodbye hug and kiss. And that your mum left gifts around the house to surprise your dad."

Drew nodded, his eyes glistening. "Yeah. I remember."

"Your mum wasn't around your whole life, but you learned what's important from her. And if you hadn't, if you'd lost your mum sooner... Lisa was wrong."

I dropped my hands from his face, hoping at least a small fraction of what I'd said would sink in.

"So... I'm doing this boyfriend thing right?"

"Yes. You're doing it right."

I placed my hand on his. He was shaking, both from the cold and the emotion. I wasn't doing any better myself, and if we stayed where we were too much longer, we'd end up frozen in place forever as a morbid statue.

"I'm so sorry. I shouldn't have pushed you and Jason together."

Drew's fingers tightened around mine. "Don't be. I'm in no rush to do it again, but I understand why you did it. Being stuck in the middle can't be much fun."

"It's not."

He brushed his hand gently across my cheek. "Thank you. For putting up with both of us for so long. Jason was right about one thing last night. We're lucky to have you."

Closing my eyes, I turned my head and planted a kiss on the palm of his hand. "I think I'm pretty lucky, too."

chapter twelve
As Appealing As A Massage from
Edward Scissorhands

The journey home was long, and would probably have felt longer if tiredness hadn't taken me. I slept for three and half hours of the five hour drive, and the time I was awake, Drew and I sat in a comfortable silence, holding hands, neither of us needing to fill the quiet with pointless chatter. When we hit the Devon/Cornwall border, I used my phone to check if Derek had made the statement to clear my name. He made it shortly after we left the hotel, and the results weren't so bad. Opinions were split, with some saying Derek was lying for me, and others defending me, saying a private argument should never have been in the news in the first place. Having some support, even from strangers, helped my mood a little and I sent Derek a text to thank him for giving it a shot. Also on the way home, I called my mum to tell her Drew and I wouldn't be joining the family for dinner. The last thing we needed was Drew and Jason in a confined space again. However, she insisted we at least show up for a quick bite to eat so I reluctantly agreed, though I wanted nothing more than to have a quiet night with Drew.

When we arrived at my flat, Drew dumped our stuff by the door. "Do you mind if I have a shower?"

He had that sleepy-eyed, *it's-been-a -long-day-and-I-need-to-wake-myself-up-again* look. What he really needed was a good night's sleep and a break from thinking.

"Help yourself. I'm gonna mess around in my workroom for a while. Come and get me when you're done."

"Okay." He kissed me on the cheek, picked up his bag and headed for the bathroom.

Letting out a long held in sigh, I went into my studio, and collapsed onto the stool beside the potter's wheel. I felt pretty groggy myself, and I needed time alone to process everything that had happened. As my brain regurgitated the events of the day, my hands picked up the huge bowl beside me, and my feet led me to the kitchen to fill it up.

I hope Jason's okay.

He'd given Drew a hard time, throwing out as many words to hurt him as he could muster. Underneath, his own sadness had begun to shine through. Drew hurt him right back, and I hadn't seen Jason so down in years. I wanted to call him, but if he wasn't home yet, it would be hard for him to talk. If he was, he might be with his dad. I didn't want to interrupt. No. I'd wait for him to call me, like he said.

My thoughts switched back to Drew, where they'd been even as I slept in the car. My dreams took me back to childhood. In my dream I saw his mum clearly. Honestly, I was never sure if I remembered her myself, or from photos I'd seen in the Brooks' house. Either way, she really did have the most beautiful smile. Short, dark hair. Slim. In my dream, she played basketball with her boys the way I did the first day I met them. She encouraged Drew, lifted Jason up to the hoop when he couldn't reach. Laughed with them, and picked them up when they fell. That was the way I'd always imagined her to be.

It was impossible to say if Drew was right. If she'd have had what was necessary to stop Jason using cocaine. If she hadn't died, would he have snorted the first line? Smoked weed? Would he have been so determined to prove he was someone special, and not just the boy whose mum was taken too soon?

None of the answers mattered. They wouldn't change what was already done. The only thing to do now was move forward, if both Drew and Jason were ready and willing.

A lump of clay rested on the potter's wheel in front of me, and I laughed to myself. It was where I always went when I needed to relax, but usually, I did so consciously. This time, lost in my musings, I'd set everything up without thinking. Instead of changing my clothes as I normally would, I threw an old apron on for better protection, then sat down, dipping my hands in the bowl of water.

"Can I play?"

I turned at the sound of Drew's voice. He stood behind me, hair still wet, and a towel around his waist.

Maybe this *is my Demi Moore/Patrick Swayze moment.*

My mouth dried out as my eyes lingered on his chest. I loved that he wasn't as self-conscious as the night before. Since he'd opened up, it was like every part of him was mine. He'd let me further inside his head than anyone had ever been, and instead of pulling away, he wanted to be closer. All the way home, I'd expected him to shut down the way he always did when life got too heavy for him. For once, he let me stay inside the head space he usually tried to lock away, and I wanted to be there. To stay close.

I nodded, and he dragged my spare stool across the room, placing it behind me. Since he was... under-dressed, he sat sideways instead of wrapping his legs around me, but his arms snaked around my waist. His chest pressed into my back, and my perfect posture slipped away, melting a little at his touch.

"So, what do I have to do?" he asked.

"Put your hands on mine."

I put my foot on the pedal, and when the ball of clay began to spin, I placed my hands firmly on the squidgy lump. Drew's hands covered mine. "What are we making?"

"I hadn't decided. Maybe a vase?"

"Sounds good. Not very manly, though."

"You don't need to worry about feeling manly while you're sitting behind me, half naked."

Drew laughed. He pressed his cheek against mine, grazing me with his stubble. "I'm wearing underwear, Ells."

For now.

"Anyway," I said, shaking my head. "Let's do this. I'll work the clay a bit, then you can take over."

I dipped my thumbs into the top of the clay to create an opening, then let my fingers run around the edge, pulling it up slowly until it looked less like a ball and more like the beginning of a work of art. I carefully took one hand away, letting Drew's left hand touch the pot while keeping it steady with my right.

"This feels weird." He started to pull back, but I trapped him in place.

"No. Don't let go. You have to be firm."

He rested his chin on my shoulder. "If this didn't *feel* so disgusting, I'd tell you to stop talking dirty. This isn't sexy at all."

"Shut up. You wanted to help."

"Sorry. What do I do now?"

"I'm going to let go, and you're going to take control."

Drew's lips brushed against my neck. "Okay, *that* was sexy."

I tipped my head back, allowing myself to relish in the feel of his kiss. Would there ever be a time I tired of his mouth on my skin? I couldn't imagine it. I wanted more. More kisses. More of him.

"Pottery isn't supposed to be sexy," I told him, with as much conviction as I could while his lips turned me into a quivering mess. "It's relaxing."

"Uh-huh," he murmured, close to my ear. "And are you relaxed?"

"Drew!" I wailed, very aware of the spinning half-vase in my hands.

I'd never hated an inanimate object more in my life.

"Okay, okay," Drew said, but I heard him trying to hold in a laugh. "I'll take control. Of the vase."

"Thank you. I'm letting go now. Keep your hands right on it, don't ease the pressure."

I slid my hand out, but the second I did, our masterpiece folded in on itself, making it look more like a deformed jug than a vase. Loose bits of clay flew across the room and splattered against the walls.

"Was I a bit too firm?" Drew asked, shifting so his legs wrapped around me from behind, and I felt his... *firmness* pressing into my back.

We'd had a rough day, and maybe we should have talked about what would happen next with Jason, the band, and keeping me out of the spotlight. Instead, we were messing around in my work room, throwing out more double entendres than a Carry On film.

It was exactly what we needed to lighten up an otherwise dark day. Talking could wait.

"Just a tad."

He grinned as I turned to face him. "Can we try again?"

Smiling, I pressed my lips against his. "I don't think you were cut out for making pottery."

I was about to wrap my arms around his neck, but stopped because of my clay covered hands.

"Sorry. You just showered, and now you're covered in muck."

"Well, if we're not... pottering anymore, I suggest we hop back in the shower and clean off."

I screwed my face up in a show of mock thoughtfulness. "Hmm, I think I can handle that. But we can't take too long. We have to get ready to go to Mum's."

Drew's lips found my neck again. "I never want to rush when I'm with you."

If I were a cartoon character, a bunch of red love hearts would have popped up all around me.

Raking my hands through his hair - I didn't care about the mess anymore, I said, "A slow shower sounds really good."

It took gargantuan effort for Drew and me to force ourselves out of the shower... and then out of bed. We could have happily delayed a family gathering for a few more days. Not because we didn't want to see them, but because the idea of Drew and Jason being in the same room was about as appealing as a massage from Edward Scissorhands.

As we walked down the path to the front door, nerves bubbled in my stomach, and from the sweatiness of Drew's palms, I knew he felt the same way.

"It's too late to back out, isn't it?" he asked, his feet slowing the closer we got.

"Way too late. Come on, it's just our parents, and Lucy, and-"

"Jason. Who thinks I'm an evil manipulator."

"He doesn't think that."

Drew looked down at me, eyebrows raised.

Okay, that was pretty much what Jason said. And more.

"Are you ready?" I asked as we reached the front step.

Drew nodded, so I opened the door and we went inside. Right away, a loud, happy scream pierced my ears, and my eighteen-year-old sister bounded up to us like an overexcited puppy, and threw her arms around us.

"You're here!" She hugged us hard, her blonde hair hitting us in the face in the process. "I'm SO happy for you. You're going to be the best couple in the whole world!"

I giggled, hugging her back, and even Drew couldn't stop himself laughing.

"Good to see you, Lucy. And thank you."

"Thank *you*! I'm going to be super popular at college tomorrow! We might get to study you."

Lucy was working towards an A-level in media studies, and having rock star friends made her an instant hit when she began the course the previous September. Adding in a sister who'd become an overnight talking point would catapult her to a whole new level of cool.

"Always nice to have your completely selfless support." I rolled my eyes.

"Oh come on, you know I'm kidding! Sort of."

Lucy dragged us into my parents' living room, where my mum and dad, Drew's dad, and Jason all sat around stiffly, straight-backed and slightly tense. It was astonishing how British everyone became when they were nervous. Anyone would have thought they were the ones who'd had a life-changing day instead of us.

"Why does it look like a budget version of Downton Abbey in here?" I asked, glancing at each of them in turn.

Michael was the first to laugh, and everyone else soon joined in. The tension dissolved, along with the stiff upper lips, and he stood up to greet us.

"Welcome home." He gave my shoulder a warm squeeze, then patted Drew on the back.

It wasn't long before Drew and I were drowning in a sea of hugs, kisses, and congratulations, and some of the hurt about not telling them about our relationship fell away. We were lucky to have such supportive families.

When Jason stepped up to hug me, I squeezed him tightly, still feeling bad about leaving him earlier. I knew I had to go but it didn't make it any easier, especially with the whole cocaine-in-the-pocket thing hanging over me. "How are you doing?" I asked.

"I'm okay. How about you?"

"Exhausted. It's been a long day."

"Yeah it has. Is Drew okay?"

"He's... Drew."

I didn't need to elaborate.

I released myself from the hug and stepped back to survey Jason properly. He looked beat. He was trying hard to act as if everything was fine, but it didn't work on me. It was another one of those times when the brothers were freakishly alike, and I could read him with no effort at all.

"Let's get through tonight," I said. "We can try to sort everything out in the morning."

Jason nodded, giving me a weak smile, but it faded, and as Drew's hand rested on my shoulder, the tension amped up around us.

"Everything okay, Ells?"

"Fine. Everything's fine!" I spoke with an unnatural brightness that made me sound nuts. I had to do something to tone down the awkwardness, though. Drew wasn't exactly glaring at Jason, but he certainly wasn't about to greet him with an apology, no matter how bad he felt. Likewise, Jason stood, tense and unblinking.

Already, being between the two of them made my heart hurt. An invisible rope circled itself around me, each end tugging me in a different direction, splitting me in half, challenging my roles as girlfriend and best friend, trying to make me choose.

"Guys." Lucy skipped to the centre of the room, commanding everyone's attention. "Can we play some games?"

God bless my baby sister. I took Drew's hand and led him away from Jason before everyone else noticed their problems. It was bad enough the three of us were suffering.

"Not tonight, Lucy," Mum said. "We invited Ellie and Drew for dinner, and they're probably too tired for games."

"Please! It's been ages since we've all been together. We should do something fun!"

She fixed her baby blues on me. She didn't need to say a word, I caved like the pushover of a big sister I was. Game nights had been a long standing tradition for us, usually with food and a few bottles of wine to console us after Lucy kicked our asses at games on her PS3.

Besides, some of us needed the distraction of a game to carry us through the evening.

"Yes! I'll get everything set up!"

Dad threw me a smile. "Hard to resist those eyes, isn't it?"

I nodded. "The men of the world are in for a load of trouble when she realises how pretty she is."

"I'm not pretty. And I'm too focused on college to think about boys."

Everyone laughed again, and Drew and I sat down on the floor since there were no seats left.

It wasn't long before Lucy fired up one of her favourite dance games, and dragged me away from Drew to "compete" against her.

"Jason." She turned to him and waved a controller in his direction. "You want some?"

I burst out laughing as she wiggled her eyebrows at him, and he gave his first genuine smile of the night. He rose to his feet. "Bring it!"

"Mum? Are you in?"

"Absolutely!"

The four of us took our positions, and when the music started, the competition began.

"You have got to be kidding me," Jason huffed. If I could have taken my eyes away from the screen, I was sure I'd have seen his arms flailing wildly. He had no co-ordination whatsoever. Singing was one thing, but keeping up with the crazy, animated movements on-screen was quite another.

"I'm too old for this!" Mum said, though she was scoring way better than Jason.

"Stop talking," Lucy swung her arm out and narrowly missed my head. "I'm concentrating!"

Nothing could stop my sister when she was getting her groove on, and as I ducked out of her way, I stumbled and bumped into the wall, ruining my near perfect score.

"Hey!" I straightened up, scrambling to get back in the game. "Not fair!"

"Suck it up, buttercup. I'm in it to win it!"

"You tell her, Luce!" Jason laughed.

A blush coloured Lucy's cheeks, but it didn't distract her from pulling out some killer moves.

Obviously, she won, with me coming in an embarrassing third, behind my mum.

Several more rounds followed, with only Michael and Drew not getting involved. Michael wasn't into it, and Drew never played dance games. Instead, they watched the rest of us, throwing out the occasional heckle for motivation. It would have been the perfect evening if Drew and Jason didn't have so much animosity between them. I couldn't tell if everyone noticed and chose to ignore it, or if I was particularly attuned because I knew how deep their feelings ran. Either way, I felt tension rise every time they caught each other's eyes.

An hour passed, and food still hadn't been ordered yet. That was enough time for the situation to become too much for me.

I needed a breather.

Excusing myself from the games, I went through to the kitchen and leaned back against the breakfast table, blowing out a breath. If I hadn't been driving, I'd have started chugging from the nearest bottle of red wine.

We shouldn't have come. I should have been more adamant we were too tired because Drew and Jason needed to be apart until they'd cooled down. There was no disguising the awkwardness and it hurt to be around them both at the same time.

"Can I hide out here too?"

I peered up as Jason rested against the counter opposite me.

"I wasn't hiding, just taking a quick time out."

"Liar. This reminds me of when your parents had that New Year's Eve party when we were kids."

"You're never going to let me forget that, are you?"

He shook his head then began to laugh. "I couldn't find you for forty-five minutes. You were hiding under your bed because the noise from the party poppers and fireworks scared you."

"I was eight years old!"

"You were a wimp!"

I could still remember how terrified I'd been of all the loud bangs. Of course, I understood the concept of New Year's Eve, but I hated the noise that came with it. I'd been right in the middle of the action when the clock hit midnight, and explosions of sound and colour scared the crap out of me, causing me to flee to my room to hide.

"I remember Drew came looking for you," I said. "And he found our feet poking out from under my bed. I was too frightened to get out from under there, so you climbed in with me. It took Drew fifteen minutes to convince me there'd be no more noise."

Our fond smiles faded a little. So many memories like that one lived on in our minds, at least until Drew outgrew us and decided I was an annoying little brat who helped lead Jason astray. Childhood was such a simple time. Kids play, then fight, then make up; often all within one day. What the hell did we know back then? Nobody told lies that could seriously hurt someone, name-calling didn't go beyond "prat," "idiot," and "stupid head." All could be forgiven with the offering of a Kit Kat, or an invitation to the next round of Tag. In adulthood, lies lingered; forgiveness was granted but nothing was ever forgotten.

"He'll come around." I moved to stand beside Jason and linked my arm through his. "The things he said earlier-"

"Were all true," Jason finished, looking down at me. "Don't try to defend it as stuff he didn't mean because he was angry. He meant every damn word."

"So did you," I pointed out. "You said plenty to him, too. Don't think he spent the rest of the day farting rainbows. He was miserable, Jason. This isn't a one way thing."

"I know." He lowered his head, lost in thought. "I think I'm gonna go home."

Way to avoid the situation a bit longer. What was the alternative though? Another hour or two making everyone else uncomfortable? Shooting dirty looks across the room, or blanking each other? This was hardly the place for another showdown.

"Are you sure?"

Jason nodded. "It's best if I go. We're all tired and we need a break."

I unlinked my arm from his and gave him a hug. "Will you be okay?"

"Ellie, come on." He gave me a reassuring smile. "You don't need to worry about me. I'll be fine."

chapter thirteen
Shattered

"Ellie. Ellie! Wake up!"

A hand prodded at my arm, and still half asleep, I slapped it away, turning over and pulling the covers around me. It was still pitch black in my room which meant it was nowhere near time to get up.

"Ellie!"

"What?" I mumbled. "I'm sleeping."

"Dad called. Jason's in hospital, we have to go. Now!"

Dad. Jason. Hospital.

Dad called. Jason hospital.

Hospital?

I blinked a few times; the duvet still covered my head. "What?"

"Ellie, please! We need to go!"

Cool air attacked my skin as the warm covers were snatched away from me.

Hospital.

I sprung into an upright position, head throbbing. "Wait. What... Why is... What the hell's going on?"

My focus cleared and Drew stood at the side of my bed, his eyes frantically begging me to get up. He'd thrown his jeans and a t-shirt on, and while I tried to fully regain consciousness, he scrambled around the room picking up my clothes.

"He fucking overdosed on cocaine!" He threw my not-long-ago-removed outfit on the bed. "I don't know anything else, Dad wasn't making sense. Jason's in hospital and we need to get there!"

The world stopped. Drew's voice came to me in slow motion. Snippets drifting in and out of my head, trying to understand.

An overdose. How did he...? I took the cocaine away. Flushed it right down the toilet. And I was with him a few hours ago. He said he was okay. Nothing to worry about.

"Ells, please. Get dressed, or I'll have to go without you."

Shaking my head, I stood up, mind racing as I put my clothes on. Too fast. Everything was happening too fast. "Tell me what you know," I said, searching for my shoes. Where the hell were my shoes? I took them off... oh, in the kitchen! Right. Where Drew and I grabbed a glass of wine before falling into bed.

Without a thought for what Jason was doing.

Shit. Was this my fault?

Drew followed me saying, "Dad found Jason in his old room, collapsed on the bed. He said he was struggling to breathe, and he told Dad he'd used cocaine. Dad called an ambulance and... Ellie *I don't know!*"

"Okay, okay." I was struggling to breathe myself. When I'd put my shoes on, I grabbed my coat and keys. "Let's go."

I managed to get us safely to the hospital without any recollection of the journey, snippets of Drew calling Derek drifting in and out of my consciousness. The whole way I kept telling myself everything would be okay. It wasn't my fault.

The words didn't ring true.

I should have let someone know what I found. Jason promised he had no intention of using, how could he go back on that?

He's an addict, Ellie. Addicts lie.

No. He wasn't lying. At least, he wasn't when he said it, but after his argument with Drew maybe...I don't know, maybe it was too much for him. I should have called him.

Stupid, Ellie!

Please. Please, God. Let Jason get through this.

Tears prickled my eyes but I blinked them away and reached for Drew's hand as we rushed through the hospital to find Michael. With every step, my legs felt heavier, my heart pounded a little harder. As we stopped to work out where we were supposed to go, Drew's phone beeped. The text message he read made all colour drain from his cheeks.

"What is it?"

"It was Dad. Jason's in intensive care." Drew turned to me. "Did I do this to him, Ells?"

His ashen face only intensified my own guilt. I'd barely looked at him since he woke me up, but now, standing with him, I could see every thought in his head. He hadn't worked through the fight with

Jason yet, and I could practically hear him telling himself he'd failed again.

My insides twisted, nausea swirling in my gut. If anyone failed it was me.

"Drew." I squeezed his hands. "No. You didn't. This is... I don't understand what happened, but you didn't do this."

He closed his eyes and took in a deep breath. "If anything happens to him, I-"

"Don't. We need to find your dad, and the doctors can tell us what's going on, okay?"

"I don't think I can do this, Ellie. The stuff I said to him earlier..." he paused, shaking his head.

Dammit, why did I let this get so out of hand? Thinking I was protecting Drew, when all I'd really done was allow Jason another chance to let him down. I didn't see it coming. I'd tried to stop their family being ripped apart any further, but if Jason didn't pull through they would be shattered into a million pieces and I was the one who let them fall.

I took a long, slow breath. "We have to do this. Together."

On wobbly legs, we hurried to the ICU, and quickly found Michael pacing around the table in the centre of the waiting area, wringing his hands.

"Dad."

Michael looked as though he'd aged twenty years, his face completely white, his eyes full of fear. He grabbed Drew and bundled him into a hug, then pulled me in too.

"I'm so glad you're here." He clung to us like he'd never let go. "Being out here on my own while Jason's-" he paused, choking on the words. Tears burned the backs of my eyes again, and I fought hard to keep them under control.

"What's happening in there?" Drew asked, taking his dad's arm and carefully leading him to a chair to sit him down.

"They think he's had a heart attack. He couldn't breathe properly, and in the ambulance he... I don't know... I don't think he stopped breathing but he wasn't responding to anything the paramedics did. They rushed him straight here and I was asked to wait. He's only been in there about five minutes, but it feels like forever."

"So they haven't told you what's going on?"

"Not yet."

"That's not good enough. They can't leave us waiting around without any information."

I recognised his tone and it never led to anything good. The last thing we needed was for Drew to direct the worst of his temper at the people who were taking care of Jason.

"Drew, sit down," I said. "At least give it a bit longer, Jason's only been in there a few minutes-"

"And they left Dad without telling him what the hell is happening! I'm going to find out what's going on."

Before any of us could stop him he barged through the double doors that presumably led to where Jason was being treated.

Michael started to rise from his seat, but I gently sat him down again. He was too weak to walk anywhere, let alone drag Drew back when he was so angry. "I'll get him. I won't be long."

I ran after Drew, through the still-swinging doors, only to crash right into the back of him. He'd stopped, his eyes fixed straight ahead.

Through a large window, doctors and nurses scurried around, checking machinery and closely observing their patient who lay flat, wires attached to his chest.

His multi-coloured hair lifeless as it splayed around him on the pillow.

Their patient. That's all Jason was to them. Another patient, another life to save. They'd work hard to save him but they didn't know him. They didn't know he was always the first to buy a round in the pub, or that he would rather bleach his own eyeballs than swallow a drink as bland as tea. They didn't know he'd started playing guitar when he was thirteen because Drew was having drum lessons, and more than anything, he wanted to be in a band with his big brother. They didn't know he couldn't play for shit, but luckily, he had a great voice.

Had. Like he wasn't alive. He didn't look alive, all limp and unresponsive. Not our full-of-life Jason.

I wrapped my arms around Drew to steady myself, the beeps of the various contraptions ringing in my ears.

"We... we shouldn't be in here," I said, my vision sliding out of focus. The stench of disinfectant that always hangs in the air in hospitals filled my nostrils stronger than ever. I grabbed at Drew's shirt, trying hard to keep my balance when I felt sure I would fall to the ground at any second.

He didn't move. Just kept staring through the window as if he couldn't hear me.

Couldn't feel me.

I had to get out.

In my rush to escape to get some air I crashed into someone else, and then stumbled back into Drew. I couldn't catch my breath enough to apologise.

"Can I help you?"

The person I'd bumped into was a young, blonde nurse who looked like she'd stepped off the set of Holby City.

"That's my brother." Drew nodded towards Jason's room. "I... I..."

"We want to know how he's doing." My voice cracked as I spoke.

A glimmer of recognition flickered in the nurse's eyes before her face fell. My sinking heart followed as she rested her hand on my arm. "I think you'll be more comfortable in the waiting room," she began, leading me towards the doors, but Drew stopped her.

"Not until you tell us what's going on."

He fixed her with his most intimidating stare, and her cheeks flushed with discomfort. "If you give me five minutes, I can-"

"You can't keep us waiting! I want to know what's happening in there!"

The nurse stepped back from the sheer force of his words. I couldn't blame her for increasing her distance. Drew was scary when he fully lost his temper, but he'd barely started, and she didn't look like someone who could handle one of his full-blown rages. I took another huge lungful of air. "Drew, cool it."

"Ellie-"

"No! Go and sit with your dad, okay?"

He glared at me, and with a frustrated growl, barged back through the doors to the waiting room.

"I'm sorry." I turned to the nurse. "It's been a rough day."

The nurse gave a weak smile. "I guess I need to get used to this kind of thing. I'm new and I haven't developed a thick skin yet." She glanced over her shoulder to Jason's room, where nurses continued to monitor him with concerned faces. "I'm also not good at not getting emotionally attached. I still get upset every time we lose someone."

Why did she look at Jason before she said that?

Catching on to my concern, she added, "Oh God, I didn't mean..." She ran a hand through her hair, still flustered. "This is totally unprofessional but... that's Jason Brooks. It's throwing me off to see a man I watched on stage a few weeks ago lying in a hospital bed, fighting for his life."

It *was* a little unprofessional, but I sort of understood. I saw women like her every time I went to a gig. Women who loved the band, felt a connection to them. This girl had the added "local" bond with them. Her forehead was creased with worry for a man she only knew from the papers, and she'd just been yelled at by a member of a band she loved.

"What's your name?" I asked.

"Natalie."

She fidgeted with the edge of her sleeve, reminding me of a small child who was about to get a telling off. I chuckled. She was obviously several years older than me, and smart enough to be a nurse. Even in such horrible circumstances there was humour in the proof that no matter what age a person is they can be brought to their knees by someone they admire.

"Natalie. If someone has to take care of my best friend, I couldn't have asked for anyone better than a fan. I know you'll make sure he gets everything he needs." I gave her hand a quick squeeze. "If you could please find someone who can tell us what's going on, we'd appreciate it."

Natalie nodded. "I'll do that right now." She smiled again, a little more brightly. "Thank you, Ellie."

My eyes widened in surprise. *How does she...?* Oh right. A fan. It would be a long time before I got used to strangers knowing my name.

"I'd better get back to Drew," I said. "Thanks for your help."

Slightly less nauseous and wobbly, I headed through the doors, to Drew and Michael. Michael still sat in the chair where I left him, but Drew was furiously pacing, and on seeing me he charged, gripping the tops of my arms. Not hard enough to hurt, but with desperation for a diagnosis.

"What did she say?"

"Nothing yet. She's going to find someone who can talk to us."

Drew threw out a string of curse words, turning away from me, but I pulled him back.

"Hey!" I placed my hands on his shoulders. "Stop shouting or you'll get thrown out."

"Ellie-"

"Drew." I linked my fingers behind his neck, giving him no choice but to look at me. I didn't need to speak, I needed him to focus on me, and I waited for him to stop throwing out venomous vibes. "Let the doctors do their job. If nobody's been out in another ten minutes, we'll go back and find someone to ask. Right now, the doctors need to be with Jason."

Eventually he nodded. "Okay. Okay. I'll go get us some coffee. Can you stay with Dad?"

"Of course."

He pressed his lips against my forehead before walking away.

Once Drew was out of sight, I sighed, and sat down beside

Michael. Trying to keep my own emotions in check was draining me of the little energy I had, without the added stress of stopping Drew from having a meltdown too. My long, unbrushed hair fell around me like a curtain, blocking out the world.

"You're really good for him, you know? Nobody else can keep his temper under control the way you can. Nobody ever could. You've always been special to him, Ellie. I'm afraid he's like his old man, though. Takes him a long time to say how he feels. I'm glad he got around to it." Michael patted my hand.

The sickness in my stomach returned. Painful, torturing. Instead of making a dash for the door like I wanted to, I turned my hand over in his and linked our fingers together.

"Thank you. That means a lot."

I only hope he feels the same way when I tell him I kept Jason's secret.

I took in a sharp intake of breath. I hadn't realised I had any intention of telling anyone I saw Jason with cocaine. I wanted to sweep it out of my mind. The guilt was already eating away at me though. What choice did I have?

When Drew returned with the coffees, he sat beside me looking a little less ready to kill someone. He rested his hand on my leg, and again, silence fell.

Barely a few minutes passed before the double doors opened, and a dishevelled doctor, roughly in his mid-fifties, gave us a warm smile as he approached. We all got to our feet, the tension building with every step he took.

"Hello, I'm Doctor Vaughan," he said, in a tone that wasn't as comforting as the smile he flashed us. I stepped closer to Drew, resting my head on his shoulder and bracing myself for what was about to come.

"I'm Michael, Jason's dad. How is he?"

Doctor Vaughan's lips pulled into a straight line before he spoke. "Lucky. He's lucky. Jason's cocaine use triggered ventricular tachycardia, which in turn, led to ventricular fibrillation just as we got him into intensive care."

He may as well have been talking a foreign language.

"I'm sorry," Michael said. "What does that mean?"

"Ventricular tachycardia is a speeding up of the heart rate, and ventricular fibrillation occurs when the heart beats become irregular, and stop the heart functioning correctly. There's only a short time to stop ventricular fibrillation from being fatal."

Again, my body sagged against Drew's at the doctor's words.

Fatal.

This was everything we'd always feared. To have it happen at a time when Jason had been so well otherwise was... it was impossible to take in.

Drew's face paled, and he collapsed down into one of the chairs, pulling me down with him, onto his lap. He held me tightly, both of us quivering against each other.

"What...how...?" Michael struggled to get his words out, and I reached out for his hand again. "Is he okay now? Is he going to be okay?"

Doctor Vaughan sighed. "It's hard to tell at this point. He's stable, and he's responding well to the treatment. But... with ventricular fibrillation, there can be some complications."

"What kind of complications?"

"There are several things which we will investigate through tests.

There's also a small risk of brain damage due to lack of oxygen to the brain. Because Jason was already here at the hospital when it happened and we stopped it quickly, the risks are minimal. But we can't rule anything out at this stage."

Hospital. Overdose. Fatal. Complications. Brain damage.

The walls seemed to close in on me again. Every spoken word was loud in my ears, but I couldn't hear their meaning. Everything distorted, everyone too close. I pushed Drew away and started running. Out. Outside to find air. Each step felt as though it happened in slow motion. The only thing reminding me it was real was the blinding pain shooting through my skull, and the sickness climbing out of my stomach.

The moment I fell through the doors into the cold, my knees gave way, and I sank to the ground, shivering.

It was easier to breathe away from the confines of the stuffy waiting room. Away from the people whose lives I might have contributed to ruining. All it would have taken was one word to Drew and this would never have happened. Or if I hadn't pushed Drew and Jason to talk, maybe it wouldn't have come to this. All logical thoughts about how, if Jason wanted to use, he would have no matter what I said or did floated around my head, but I couldn't shake the guilt. Earlier, Jason said the dealer practically lined the coke up for him. I didn't ever expect to feel like I'd done the same thing.

"Ellie."

Drew's arms raised me from the ground, then firmly secured me in a hug that threatened to crack my ribs. I didn't care. I needed it. Needed to feel the comfort before I told him the truth and maybe ruined everything between us before we'd really got started.

"I'm sorry I ran out."

His hand burrowed inside my hair. "It's okay, Ells. We're going home now."

"Home?" I asked, pulling away. "But... aren't we going to stay with your dad?"

Drew shook his head. "He wants to be alone for a while."

"What else did the doctor say?"

"Nothing much. We just have to wait. Jason's better, but there still aren't any guarantees he'll make it through the night."

"That's more reason for us to stay! If something happens to him-"

"Ellie, I can't." His gaze dropped. "Dad said he'll call if anything happens but I can't wait around here. It's too much."

I spent the drive home trying to figure out how to tell Drew I knew about Jason craving cocaine. Then trying to talk myself out of it. *Should I drop this on him when Jason's life is hanging in the balance?* Drew felt responsible. I wanted to take the burden from him because it wasn't his to carry. It was mine, at least in part. There was no 'good' option. Either way, it would result in more pain for Drew.

And what about Jason? From the minute Drew woke me, I'd stopped thinking about Jason as a person. My brain flicked into some weird preparation mode, readying me in case the worst happened. All normal human emotion disappeared, and while I was still terrified about whether or not he'd make it, I felt disconnected. From him, and from the situation. I knew for sure, if he could, Jason would tell me to keep my mouth shut but he once had lying down to a fine art. That wasn't me.

It was after two a.m. when we arrived back at my flat. Instead of a comfort, the silence was eerie. That strange stillness you feel when something big is happening, and you know the world is turning the same as always, but your own has stopped, waiting for the next piece of news.

Drew hadn't uttered a word since we left the hospital. I didn't need to ask what he was thinking; it was all there on his exhausted face. I couldn't recall ever seeing him so afraid, but that wasn't everything. A glimmer of anger lurked in his eyes, contributing to his guilt. I'd seen it so many times. I'd felt it myself. How could Jason keep doing this to himself, to us? And how could we be mad at him when he was suffering too?

"Thanks, Ellie."

Drew's voice startled me.

"What for? I was no help whatsoever. I ran away."

"You stopped me knocking that nurse's head off. You kept me calm. You kept Dad calm. You didn't blame me for this when we both know I had something to do with it."

I shook my head. "No. You didn't."

"He was fine until I laid into him. This isn't a coincidence."

"He wasn't fine, Drew. You must have seen that while you were fighting. He was hurting before you said a word."

"Then I pushed him. I pushed him into this, and-"

"Stop." I reached up, cupping his face in my hands. "This wasn't your fault."

My thumbs lightly ran across his stubble as the weight pressing down on me pushed harder. *Those eyes.* They stared into mine, searching for answers. Searching to see if I meant what I said.

"Drew-"

I was cut off when his lips crushed against mine. The stubble that a second ago had been beneath my fingers, grazed my cheeks and chin. He grabbed at my hips, gathering me in.

"Wait." I rested my hands against his chest, trying to catch the breath he'd stolen from me. "I need to tell you-"

"No more talking."

His mouth bore down on mine again, body reacting faster than brain. His tongue pushed against my lips, and I let him in, letting him closer when I needed to step back, to think. Impossible when he held me against him, stealing my self-control with every touch of his lips. He'd never been like this before. Enthusiastic and hot as hell? Yes. But never with so much desperation, like the world was going to end and this was the way he wanted to spend his last moments. I loved it. Wanted it.

Jason's lying in a hospital bed. You helped put him there.

I wriggled out of Drew's arms. Jesus. My body still trembled from his touch while my mind insisted on thinking rationally. I wanted to smack myself for breaking away, or maybe for giving in when I needed to talk to him. Either way, I was frustrated as hell.

"How can you want to do this right now? After everything that's happened."

Drew buried his hand deep in my hair. "I need you, Ellie. Right now, I really need you."

He kissed me again. More softly, but still with a desperation that screwed with my self-control. His pain hit full force, mixing with my own, causing tears to form in my eyes. Lips brushed against my eyelids, cheeks, the tip of my nose, along my jawline.

"Please," he whispered. "Please."

As the first tear dropped, I moved closer, taking his face in my hands again. Nothing more needed to be said. This time, when he kissed me, I responded with equal intensity, tugging at his shirt because he wasn't close enough.

Couldn't get close enough.

I didn't realise how much I needed him, needed this. To lose myself in him, and let him lose himself in me. Everything we felt became fuel for our hands to tear at each other's clothes, pulling and ripping. Instead of heading to my room, Drew shuffled me towards the living room, our clothes leaving a pervy Hansel and Gretel trail behind us as they dropped to the floor.

Well, this is new.

When Drew lifted me up onto the edge of the dining room table, only our underwear remained intact; doubts were nothing more than a distant memory. He unhooked my bra and tossed it across the room; hungry lips found my breasts, stubble scratching hard against my skin. As Drew's mouth continued its assault, I slipped my hands inside his boxers, tugging them down and thrusting my hips forward, feeling how much he wanted me. Heat shot through me as he gave a low, primal growl. I raked my fingers through his hair then pulled him up to me, needing his mouth on mine.

God, I loved the way he felt under my hands, the way he responded to my every move, the salty sweat on his skin.

Tender kisses turned to animalistic need. From the force of Drew's fingers digging into my flesh, I was sure I'd be bruised in the morning.

I didn't care. Being wanted this way, this much, lit a fire in me. I nipped at his neck and shoulder with my teeth and he firmly held my hips, lifting me up just enough to rip my knickers off, pull me towards him, and thrust inside me, our eyes connecting.

My pulse spiked. Behind the intense expression so familiar to me, something else shone through. A wildness, like a caged tiger that had been set free; free to roam, to explore. To claim.

I moaned, loud and desperate, clamping my legs around him, pressing my hips against his and burying my head against his shoulder. As he brought me closer and closer to the edge, I refused to fall, not yet, *not yet*. I bit harder, trying to hold on; making him growl again, making him push harder until neither of us could stop the waves any longer.

Cries of pleasure, cries of *relief*, bounced off the walls around us, echoing through me as my shaking, sweaty body sagged against Drew's. Weak, but so damn satisfied.

Without a word, Drew scooped my trembling form from the table, and carried me to my room. Carefully, he pulled back the duvet, and lowered me onto the cool, crisp sheets before climbing in beside me and gathering me in his arms again, softly kissing my forehead.

"Are you okay?" he whispered.

"No," I mumbled into his chest. "Wanna do it again."

"I didn't hurt you?"

"No." I closed my eyes, allowing my flesh to recall every lash of his tongue, the burn of his stubble. I still felt the imprint of his hands pressing into my skin and I wanted to wail out loud from how good it felt to let him take control, to do exactly what he wanted.

"Ells?"

"Mmhmm?"

"Are you sure?"

I tilted my head a little, peering up at him from beneath my eyelashes. "You didn't hurt me."

Concern melted away from his eyes, leaving them warm, soft. A million miles from the feral blaze that burned through me earlier. I smiled, neither of us needing to say any more. I could have told him I loved him, told him how lucky I was to have a best friend and a man who could make my head spin rolled into one sexy package. How I couldn't imagine being without him.

I didn't say any of those things. I knew he heard me above the noise of everything else that had happened that day. There was no need for words.

chapter fourteen

A Particularly Rough Game of
British Bulldog

Morning brought good news. Jason had woken up shortly after we left the hospital, with no brain damage, and no lasting damage to his heart. He was, however, experiencing the "coke crash," and it was sort of an unspoken agreement that, whether he wanted to or not, he would be going back to rehab as soon as possible.

Drew had been quiet since we woke up curled in each other's arms. He was being extra gentle with me; his touches light and his kisses soft, as if he trying to make up for being rougher than usual the night before. My insistence that I was fine hadn't trickled into his brain yet, in part because he had other things on his mind, and in part because he was, well, Drew.

After Michael called to tell us Jason would be fine, Drew retreated farther into his silence. Not in a blocking me out kind of way. More pensive, and trying to come to terms with everything. It scared me that I didn't know what he was thinking, but physically, he kept me close, and that was enough for me.

Our sense of happiness about Jason's diagnosis shattered in an instant when Drew and I arrived at the hospital.

The entrance was swarming with reporters.

We pulled into the car park as my phone started to ring. After some sloppy parking, I cast my eyes down at the screen. Mum.

"Deja vu, anyone?" I gave a weary sigh,

"We should start getting papers delivered. That way we'll know what we're doing at the same time as everyone else."

With a grimace, I clicked the answer button.

"Hi, Mum."

"Ellie! Have you seen the newspapers?"

This is fast becoming my least favourite phrase.

"No, but we're at the hospital and there are cameras and journalists everywhere."

"They know *everything.* About the... the cocaine."

Mum's stutter over the word "cocaine" didn't surprise me at all. Open-minded as she was, and as much as she cared for Jason, his drug use had always frightened her. At his worst; stealing, and punching anyone who got in the way of his next fix, she'd been afraid he'd show up at the house, asking for money to fund another hit. One night, while visiting his dad, Mum found him talking to Lucy over the fence, completely off his head. Lucy was only fifteen at the time, and Mum rushed her away in case he flipped out. Not that she'd ever seen him flip, but she'd heard plenty. She'd told me she felt guilty and stupid for being afraid of Jason, who she'd watched grow up. I could hardly judge her for her fears. A lot of the time, I'd felt the same way.

This time was different, though. This was *not* going to be another dramatic slide back to how he used to be.

"All the quotes come from a source," Mum went on. "No names. But they know Jason could have died."

I imagined Derek had planned another cover-up story, but since the truth had already leaked out, any tale he'd concocted would be rendered useless. This kind of press was the last thing the band needed so close to hitting the big time, and Derek would have to implement some serious damage control to save their reputation.

Luckily, he'd had a lot of practise in that area.

"Anything else I should know?"

A pause. "Why aren't you more upset about this?"

"Well, I can't say I'm happy, but... Jason's okay. That's the most important thing right now."

"True," Mum said, concern still strong in her voice. "Ellie, I hate this world you've been dragged into."

"I hate it, too especially because I know how much you worry. But I promise I won't get lost in it. Once Jason's out of hospital, we can all move on."

I have to believe that.

Beside me, Drew tensed, and I reached for his hand. "Mum, I've got to go. Thanks for the warning. I'll give you a call later."

After I hung up, I turned to Drew. "Did you catch all that?"

He nodded. "Everyone knows."

"Yeah. But *how?*"

Drew let out a humourless laugh. "We aren't important enough to have our phones bugged, so my guess is, some underpaid doctor or nurse decided to make a bit of cash on the side by selling a story on the local rock star."

My mind leapt to Natalie, the nervous nurse, but I quickly dismissed the idea. She was afraid of her own shadow and she loved Razes Hell, especially Jason. She'd never have risked getting on the wrong side of Drew's temper again, or damaging the reputation of her favourite band. Drew had a point, though. If neither of us, or Michael, had talked to the press, there was nobody else left but hospital staff who had the full story. Even Derek didn't know everything yet.

"That's a sackable offence." *Also another reason not to think Natalie blabbed. Someone recently-ish qualified wouldn't risk throwing her hard work away for a few quid.*

"Yeah. Not a big problem when they choose to be anonymous."

I nodded towards the salivating journalists at the hospital doors. "How are we supposed to get through that lot?"

"Quickly, and heads down."

I gave him a small smile. "Are you ready?"

He shook his head, and I touched his lips with mine. "I'll be with you the whole time. I promise."

"I know."

Those words held so much. Worry, relief, gratitude. Drew pressed his cheek against mine. "I love you."

"I love you, too."

After a minute or two, Drew slowly straightened up. "Okay. Let's do this."

He hopped out of the car to pay the extortionate parking fee, and when he'd firmly placed the ticket in the window, I got out too, locking up behind me. With one last look at each other to check we really were ready, Drew wrapped his arm around me, pinning me to his side. Heads pointed to the ground, we walked quickly towards the entrance.

"Hey, there he is!"

Bright flashes hit my eyes, though I hadn't looked up. Hands grabbed, elbows jostled, shouts of, "Drew!" and, "What can you tell us about Jason?" and, "Is it true he overdosed on cocaine?" assaulted my ears. We reached the automatic doors relatively unscathed, and tumbled through, like a particularly rough game of British Bulldog, while the hospital security pushed the journalists back.

"Don't turn around," Drew said, as flashes continued to go off behind us. "Keep walking."

As we headed to the ICU, where Jason would stay until he was well enough to be transferred to a ward, Drew fell silent again, clinging to my hand.

Michael greeted us with a smile, a dramatic difference to the way he'd met us several hours before. He was clearly exhausted, but the happiness on his face knowing Jason would be okay helped disguise the dark circles under his eyes.

"Morning," he said as we approached.

"Good morning," I answered. "How are you?"

He let out a heavy sigh. "Much better than last night. Thanks for getting here so quickly."

"You need some rest, Dad. We came early so you can go home and sleep. Ellie and I will stay for a while."

Michael patted Drew's arm. "Thank you."

"Before you go, I should tell you there's a bunch of reporters outside."

"Yeah, I was warned a few minutes ago. I wish they hadn't found out about this."

"Me too. And I'm sure Derek does."

"I should call him," Drew said. "He's probably already on his way down here, though."

I couldn't help but feel a bit sorry for the band's manager. He'd had to sort out more mess in the last two days than he had the whole time he'd worked with the guys.

"Oh! Do Mack and Joey know what happened? For real, I mean, not what's in the papers."

Through the panic, I'd kind of forgotten about the other members in the band.

"Derek rang them last night. I should probably phone them, too." Drew pulled out his mobile, and started to turn back towards the corridor.

"Wait." Drew halted in his tracks. "Don't you want to see Jason first?"

He lowered his head, and I was sure Michael would tell Drew to put his phone down and visit his brother. Instead, he threw me a warm smile and patted Drew's arm. "I'll leave you to it. I'll be back in a few hours."

As he walked away, I wondered if Jason had told him about the fight between him and Drew. And if he hadn't, how much did Michael really know? I suspected he knew a whole lot more about his sons' issues than he let on, but I couldn't judge him for not pushing it.

"I'm still not ready," Drew said once Michael had gone. "I don't think I want to see him yet."

"Why not?"

"You know why not."

I took his free hand. "Look at me."

Drew raised his head, his eyes meeting mine.

"I understand how you feel. I do. But he's your brother, and last night we weren't sure we'd ever get to talk to him again."

I choked on the words, momentarily transported back to the time there was a very real possibility Jason wouldn't get through the night.

I saw all of Drew's anger and guilt, just as I did the night before. My stomach twisted, reminding me of my own part in this mess and I swallowed hard to shift the dryness in my throat. "Shall we go to the canteen for a drink before we do this?"

"No. Why don't you go in and see Jason, I'll make the calls, and then... I'll be ready."

He didn't give me time to argue the point. He left me in the waiting area while he shot away to phone Derek. I couldn't blame him for prolonging this. Beyond the relief Jason was on the mend, the rest of Drew's issues hadn't been resolved. How could they be when he hadn't talked about it, and he certainly hadn't been able to talk to Jason?

With a sigh, I pushed through the double doors, and stepped into the area that had scared the hell out of me the night before.

Natalie was leaving Jason's room, and when she spotted me, her 'bunny in the headlights' look crossed her face again. "Ellie, I hoped I'd see you today. I wanted to tell you it wasn't me who talked to the press, but I think it was someone from here. We all got called to a staff meeting this morning and they are doing everything they can to find out who did it. I was worried you'd assume it was me because of the way I acted last night, and I didn't want you to think-"

A small giggle escaped my lips. Again, she'd somehow made me laugh in the most serious of situations. How the heck did she make it through university, watching disgusting videos of... whatever medical students have to endure to complete their studies, if she panicked over every tiny thing?

"Natalie, I didn't think it was you."

Her shoulders dropped from their hunched, tense position. "Thank you."

"Did you talk to Jason about this?"

"No. People who have had heart problems aren't supposed to be stressed out in any way. I decided I'd speak to you because... Drew scares me."

Again, I laughed out loud. His height and build never intimidated me, but based on the way he'd spoken to her before, I understood her reluctance to talk to him again. "He's a big teddy bear. Really."

A shadow of doubt crossed her face. "He was more like a grizzly bear last night." Catching herself, she added, "Sorry."

"It's fine. How is Jason doing?"

"Heart-wise, he's doing brilliantly. Cocaine-wise... he's okay. A bit jumpy and down in the dumps but it's to be expected after what he went through. We're going to move him out of intensive care this afternoon and up to a ward where there'll be people around all the time. Hopefully being in a room with others will help a bit."

Depressed Jason was not the best person to be with. I wondered how much of his mood was actual withdrawal, and how much was him tormenting himself over what he did.

"Thanks, Natalie."

She gave my arm a comforting squeeze before heading away to check on her other patients, and I took a deep breath and opened the door to Jason's room.

He sat, propped up by pillows, his head turned to one side, and his eyes closed. He wasn't asleep; his fingers drummed on the mattress. He was still hooked up to a couple of machines monitoring his heart rate, but the picture was a lot less horrifying than the one I'd witnessed a few hours earlier.

"Hey."

Jason's eyes sprung open, fingers halting the rhythm they'd been pounding. He didn't say a word, surveying my face for some indication of whether I was going to hug him or slap him. Before I'd opened the door, I hadn't figured out the answer myself. But, dammit, he was here, he was alive.

I ran my hand across my forehead, easing away an ache that erupted from nowhere. Maybe I was *still* undecided.

Feelings are never straightforward when an addict is involved. When someone you care about does something so damaging, it changes the way you see them. Not completely, because you cling to the hope they'll sort themselves out, and you hang on to all the memories you had of them before they changed. In the end, that was what always drove me mad. Seeing those glimpses of the real Jason; him playing on them as a way to gain some understanding before he stole money from my purse, CDs from my collection, and a necklace my grandma gave me before she died.

I knew this was different. A different time, and a different... meaning, I guess. But the damage had still been done. He'd found a reason to use, and it almost killed him.

Moisture formed behind my eyes, and I shook my head, keeping my focus on him. Happiness and disappointment, and that awful, nagging guilt crashed over me, pulling me in so many different directions. I wanted to curl up into a ball and wait for it all to pass so I didn't have to deal with it. Didn't have to be the one in the middle, trying to cope with everyone else's feelings as well as my own.

"Come here." Jason reached out to me.

My feet carried me towards him though my brain wasn't quite sure. As his fingers closed around mine, I sank onto the bed, resting my head in his lap as tears dripped onto his blankets.

"Ellie, I'm so sorry."

Words lodged in my throat as I tried to tell him never to scare us like that again. He seemed to understand. I felt his tears falling on me. Eventually, I straightened up so I could look at him.

"I'm supposed to yell at you."

Jason nodded, his eyes lacking their usual sparkle. In fact, looking at him closely, everything about him was missing its shine. His purple streaked hair was lifeless and faded. On a normal day, he oozed charisma, but this was far from an ordinary day. It was as if a switch had flicked off, snuffing out his drive to succeed. A broken soul.

"You should yell at me, I deserve it. What I did last night was the stupidest thing I've ever done."

"So why did you do it? And where did you get the drugs?"

He shuffled awkwardly in his bed. "I called the bloke from the club and got him to meet me before we left London."

My eyebrows shot upwards. "You kept his number?"

A small nod answered my question and I stood up, head pounding from dehydration after all the tears I cried. "You said you had no intention of using again! Why would you keep a dealer's number if you weren't planning to use? Was everything you told me a load of crap?" I asked, pacing the room.

"No." He lowered his eyes. "When I told you I wasn't planning to use, I meant it."

"But you still had his number! If you'd wanted my help, you'd have let me delete it at the same time I flushed the drugs he gave you!"

"I thought I could do it myself, okay? I thought once the coke was gone, I could take the next step alone. But then... after arguing with Drew and being at your parents' house..." he trailed off.

I clenched my jaw. If he'd dared to lay the blame for his slip-up at Drew's feet, I would have swung for him.

"Why didn't you ring me?"

"Why do you think? Drew was already pissed off with me. I didn't want to-"

"He's not an ogre! If you'd told him what was going on-"

"He'd have had me back in rehab before I'd finished getting the words out!"

"Well you're going back now anyway, so what bloody difference does it make? I lied for you, Jason! I risked everything because I trusted you, and look where we are!"

Another stream of tears fell from Jason's eyes, and the throbbing in my head intensified. How did he not understand? How could he think Drew would ever want to see him suffer?

The same way Drew thinks Jason doesn't respect him.

They were so close once. When they were kids, through their teen years, right up to the day Jason started lying about his drug use. They patched up the damage afterwards, but it all came back when the stupid feud dredged up whatever unresolved feelings lurked under the surface, and tore open old wounds, making them bleed out onto everyone around them.

Mostly onto me.

"I miss her too, you know?"

My head snapped up. "What?"

"My mum," he whispered. "I miss her."

Deep inside my chest, my heart quivered, shooting out waves of grief for him that surged through my veins, making me clutch at my stomach.

As if that would make it stop.

I knew it. I knew that was the comment that tipped Jason over the edge. Any reference to their mother was extremely rare because the whole family was always so concerned they might upset each other. It wasn't like she never existed, but it certainly wasn't a topic they approached without a reason. Didn't other families occasionally mention the person they missed, reminiscing about old times and keeping the memories alive?

"Drew said Dad blamed himself for not doing enough for me after Mum died. So, I went to Dad's after I left your parents' house and waited for him to come home. I wanted to tell him he did. He did more than enough. It wasn't his fault I turned out this way. It was all me."

"Did you tell him?"

Jason nodded. "Yeah. And it was the first time I felt as though I'd spoken to him properly in years. We talked about Mum, and... I told him I can't remember her. Not clearly. All I have are these stupid snippets of events that might never have happened. The memory of her teaching me and Drew to ride our bikes in the back garden. Consoling me after Dad told me off for messing around in his shed. Seeing her lying in her hospital bed, too weak to talk, but still managing to smile when me and Drew went to visit her."

I stepped towards him again as he paused, drawing in a shuddering breath.

"All that stuff happened. I didn't make any of it up, but I missed out on so much. She wasn't here the first time I got an A at school. She wasn't around to give me a lecture about not breaking girls' hearts. Didn't see our first gig. So, last night, I went up to my old room at Dad's house so I could think about everything. Mum, Drew, you." He shook his head. "I never dealt with any of that stuff properly. Not even in rehab. I sound like a fucking cliché, because you know what? My life didn't turn out so bad. But I hid behind drugs, and last night, just for once, I used the coke knowing I couldn't blame anyone but myself. Not Mum for dying when I was young, not Dad for not being enough, not Drew for always being on my case, and not you for being so damn reasonable all the time."

"Jason," I whispered. "Did you overdose on purpose?"

His eyes widened. "What? God, Ellie, no. No. I didn't want to die. I wanted to... I don't know... escape."

It wasn't a good enough excuse. Nothing justified him using cocaine again, but how could I be angry with him? Seeing him in so much pain made me ache. For what he'd lost and for all the issues he'd kept inside for way too long. He hadn't gotten low enough to want to end it all, but if he'd continued feeling like he had nowhere to turn? What then?

My head gave another painful throb, and I squeezed my eyes shut.

Just a bit longer, Ellie. Then you can go get some air. And painkillers.

I didn't want to leave until Drew arrived and I'd ensured there was no danger of them fighting again. They'd both been hurt enough.

"I want to go to rehab," Jason said, surprising me.

He hated that place.

"You know that decision's already been made?"

He gave a small laugh through his tears. "I know. But I want to go. Ellie, you have to understand, if I hadn't used, I'd still have had that need in me. If you'd told Drew, or if you'd checked me into rehab yourself, I would have gone in, listened without hearing, and come straight back out and done what I intended to do all along. Rehab takes work. You know who I am, you've always known. I'm an addict, and we can be as devious we need to be until we get what we want. I never meant for you to get involved, and I'm sorry you did. But maybe this had to happen, to scare me into getting clean for good."

His words did nothing to ease my guilt, even though a part of me knew he was right. It would have taken more than a few rounds of pyschobabble to make Jason stop when he'd set his mind on something. I'd seen him steal from his family, from my family, heard him tell lie after lie just so he could get a fix. Even now, with so much conviction in his voice, there were no guarantees he would never relapse.

"I want my life back, Ellie. I want to get back with the band and-"

"Slow down." I sat beside him again. "There's a long way to go yet. A lot of recovery. And...while we're being honest, Jason, I have to tell Drew the truth. That I knew you had cocaine on you yesterday."

"Ellie, no. I'm not saying this for me, I'm saying it for you. He won't understand what you did. You can't tell him."

"I have to. How are we supposed to fix everything if there's a huge lie in the way?"

"What lie?"

Jason's face paled, his gaze focusing over my shoulder.

This is fine; you were going to tell him anyway, weren't you?

That didn't stop my heart from forgetting to beat at the sound of Drew's voice. I *was* going to tell him, but away from the hospital to limit the amount of people who'd hear the fallout.

I rose from the bed, already knowing what I'd see. Drew's jaw clenched, his chest rising and falling faster than normal, and his eyes flicking from me to Jason.

"It's nothing. Right, Ellie?"

Wrong.

"What do you need to tell me the truth about, Ellie?"

The feeling of weight pressing down on me, stealing my breath bore down on me again, and mixing in with my hammering head, I could easily have sunk to my knees, crying because I didn't know what to do.

You know what to do.

"There's something I should have told you yesterday."

"Ellie," Jason said. "Don't. Please."

We both knew what would happen when the words came out, and again, my chest ached, my insides shrivelling away to nothing. Bits of me seemed to be slowly dying, like petals falling from a wilting flower. There was only one way Drew would see this.

"Yesterday morning, when you left me and Jason to talk, he had cocaine in his pocket."

For the briefest second, Drew's jaw relaxed, his eyes softening. It passed in a flash, though. When my words filtered through to his brain, he tilted his head to one side. "What?"

What did he think I was going to say? Jason and I had decided to take a trip back to the days of our beer-goggled kisses, and spent the morning dry humping in my hotel room?

Actually, that was probably it, which would have infuriated me under different circumstances. Pretty hard to be angry with someone when you've played right into their insecurities.

"He had cocaine on him, and you *knew*?"

"It wasn't her fault," Jason said, and I turned to him. "I asked her to help me, and she flushed it but I made her promise not to tell you. I didn't plan to use again, and Ellie-"

"Jason, stop," I interrupted, turning back to Drew. "That *is* what happened, but I should have let you know."

"Why didn't you?" he asked, his voice frighteningly stoic.

"Because I-" I paused, taking a careful step closer to him. "I believed him when he told me it was a one-off. He hadn't used any, and I thought once I got rid of what he had, it would be over. I realise it was stupid of me, but yesterday was such a huge mess, and I wanted-"

"To lie to me, and risk Jason getting hooked on that crap again?"

"No! I didn't *want* to lie to you, but I didn't want to make things worse between you two, either. I was scared one more thing would make everything blow up again and I couldn't stand the thought of you reaching a point where you might not... you might not ever be able to fix your relationship."

It sounded like such a flimsy reason, since we were all in the local hospital after a near-death situation. The reality slammed into me, reinforcing what a complete idiot I was to think Jason could have handled what he was going through alone. I'd made a decision in the moment, knowing the risks and landed us right in "worst case scenario" territory.

"I didn't plan to use, but you-"

"Don't!" Drew snapped, his eyes igniting with fire – and not the good kind. "Don't you dare blame me for this!"

"I wasn't going to. But yeah, having you remind me what a fuck up I am didn't make my day any easier. I'm saying Ellie believed me because I told her the truth at the time."

"You both should have known better! You should have admitted you needed help, and Ellie should have come to me if you were too stubborn to do it yourself!"

"Stop!" I shouted. "Both of you stop!"

I couldn't take another round of them tearing strips off each other. Not when my heart was already cracking apart in my chest. Drew's refusal to look at me was torture. I needed him to acknowledge me, to hear me, to understand I didn't make my decision lightly. It hurt, and I hated it but at the time, it seemed like the best thing to do.

He was right there. My man. Then tears prickled my eyes because maybe he wasn't mine anymore. The lips I'd kissed, the hands that knew every curve of my body, the soft stomach I'd snuggled into, and the warmth of him when he pressed up against me. I was losing it all.

"Drew. I didn't... I didn't-"

"I don't want to hear it, Ellie. You made your choice. Looks like I was right all along."

Some kind of spasm erupted in my chest as he walked away, and I wanted to scream. At the pain. The unfairness of his last words. Because, dammit, hadn't I showed him he was everything? Hadn't I laid everything out there and been patient while he tried to work through his own feelings? I'd listened without judging, my heart aching anytime he was in pain, and he was tossing it all aside.

My mistake wasn't small, I understood that. It symbolised every fear he had that somewhere deep inside, Jason was who I really wanted. That Jason and I would always have memories he wasn't a part of. But it *was* a mistake, one I'd do everything to fix if he'd only listen.

"Ellie. If you've got a chance to make this right, it's now. Before he overthinks it and turns it into something way more meaningful than it is."

I whipped my head around to look at him, and on seeing the sparkle of tears in his eyes, my own spilled. I covered my eyes with my forearm, as if the action would block everything out.

It still hurt just the same.

"Ellie, come on," Jason urged. "Go now. I know I acted like a dick about it yesterday, but this, you and Drew, it's right."

"He isn't going to get over this."

"He won't get over it if you don't try."

I threw my head back, wishing I knew the magic words to make Drew hear me. Instead, frustration filled me because the right words didn't exist. Jason was right, though. If I didn't try to fight for him, for us, he'd keep on thinking he was right. The part of his head that couldn't let go of anything, ever, would get the best of him.

Charging out of Jason's room, I hoped Drew hadn't gotten too far. My legs felt like noodles, unstable and barely able to carry my weight as I hurried down the corridors, twisting my neck left and right, searching for him through blurry eyes.

There.

The back view of him disappeared into the cafeteria, and I picked up my speed, hoping my legs would hold out a little longer.

I didn't want a showdown in a public place; I'd been a victim of camera-happy observers more than enough times over the past couple of weeks. Thankfully, there weren't too many people in the canteen besides a few exhausted-looking visitors, and a couple of nurses grabbing coffee.

"Drew," I said, gasping for breath.

I didn't dare touch him, even though every part of me screamed out to circle my arms around him in the hope it would ease his pain a little.

When he turned to me, I was looking at the Drew from a few weeks ago. The one who could shut off his emotions at the snap of his fingers, and not only deny any feelings for me, but stare at me as if I was a stranger.

I blinked, trying to get rid of the tears. "Drew, I'm so sorry. Please, can we talk?"

"I've already heard everything I need to. You lied to me. You covered for Jason, and he nearly died."

It really was that simple for him. He could pick and choose which parts he wanted to listen to, neatly lock them away in compartments in his brain to stew over later. Okay, when it came down to it, that was the truth. I didn't need any reminders of how stupid I was, because he was right. I should never have kept the truth from him. But my reasons? They weren't selfish. I didn't do it for me, or for Jason, but for the brothers. To stop them ruining all they'd worked for.

I wanted to say it out loud, but I couldn't get more than a squeak to leave my lips.

Drew started to walk away, and I reached out with trembling hands to pull him back, my fingers closing around his wrist. His gaze focused on the point where I touched him, but he didn't pull away. He didn't move at all.

"Please, don't do this. Don't shut me out. I need you to listen to me."

"I needed *you* to tell me the truth but you didn't!"

"I tried to tell you last night."

"Last night was too late!" he snapped, and I started to feel the now familiar sensation of people turning to stare. His voice lowered. "Let go of me."

I shook my head, staring up at him, willing him to look at me. My breath came out in small, ragged gasps as I fought to keep from breaking down. I was losing him, but if I kept my hand on his wrist, he was still there, still mine. He had to tell me it was okay.

Had to.

The man I'd waited so long for couldn't leave me this way. Hanging on, needing to hear him say he understood.

"Ellie."

One word. That was all it took to break my heart. His eyes locked onto mine.

"You need to go now."

"No." I gripped his arm tighter, desperately shaking my head. "Drew."

"Ellie, stop."

His hand covered mine, and for a second, he gently squeezed. It was only for a moment, but it filled me with warmth, like always.

Don't move. Please. Let me have this moment to fool myself we're going to be okay. Please.

His eyes closed, then prised my fingers from him. "I'll see you around."

As he walked away, he heaved a sigh and quickly brushed his hand across his face while I stood, frozen.

I was aware of the people around me, whispering, watching and that was enough to make me will my feet to move, even though all I wanted was to stay close to Drew. Walking out meant admitting it was over. I *knew* it was over, but I wasn't ready to leave him behind.

See you around. Like we were friends. Less than friends. Just two people who grew up beside each other, but hadn't shared anything. Not secrets, not worries, not even a damn cup of sugar.

And certainly not love.

My knees buckled, but I made myself walk faster through the corridors with my head down. The press were still outside the hospital entrance, but I pushed through them, hardly feeling or hearing them this time, and ran to my car, locking myself inside.

Silence surrounded me, heavy and oppressive. Pressing my forehead against the steering wheel, huge, body-wracking sobs spilled out of me, emptying me from the inside, making me hollow.

chapter fifteen
Over

I wandered into my flat in an exhausted daze. I'd walked out of the hospital more than an hour ago, but after stopping to let my tears out, then calming myself down enough to drive, plus the travel time... it seemed like ages ago since I left.

Right away, I wanted to run straight back out of the apartment.

Drew's bag from our trip to London waited in the hallway; the front pocket slightly open, the flap hanging down like a tongue poking out, mocking me. I threw my keys down on the table beside the door and went to the kitchen, giving the bag a swift kick as I walked by. It fell with a satisfying thud. I then took a bottle of water from the fridge, downing it before grabbing another and carrying it to my room.

The smell of Drew hit me immediately. The scent of his shower gel, his clothes, and... *him* clung to my bedroom.

With the little energy I had left, I crawled onto the bed, clinging to the t-shirt he'd left behind as if it was a security blanket, except secure was the last thing I felt.

I reached out and pulled my duvet around my shivering body, hiding myself away from everything. Everything but Drew's T-shirt which I clutched to my chest as if it was him. I closed my eyes. Pictured him beside me. Imagined his warm arms enveloping me, maybe brushing my hair off my face and placing a gentle kiss on my forehead. Telling me to have sweet dreams. And I'd tuck my head under his chin, pull him closer, and wrap my arms around his back.

His shirt was a lousy substitute, but it was all I had.

All I'd ever have.

There was nothing in his eyes the last time he looked at me. Like his final words, they were empty. So I focused on the one thing he gave me. The tiny, over-in-a-flash hand squeeze. If it hadn't been so tragic, I'd have laughed. Lying on my bed, cuddling Drew's shirt and trying not to lose the sensation of his hand on mine before he ripped it away. I was pathetic, and I didn't care.

Sometime between me cocooning myself in my duvet, and the sound of my phone ringing, I fell asleep. It was late afternoon when I woke up, but I didn't rush to answer the call. Instead, I lifted my face off my damp pillow, finally let go of Drew's shirt, and waited for the grief to creep over me again. The numbness of sleep made the pain go away, but with open eyes, the ache spread from my chest outwards to the tips of my fingers and toes. I threw my head back, telling myself not to cry anymore. Hard to do when everything hurt.

There's always a second when you wake up after a horrible event when you can trick yourself into believing it was a bad dream. Reality set in way too quickly, and Drew's face flickered into my mind as though a light switch had been thrown on. Was he still at the hospital? Did he talk to Jason? Did he talk to anyone? Desperation to see him clawed at my insides, reminding me we were done. Over.

I snapped out of my foggy-mindedness at the sound of my phone bleeping. To stop another waterfall streaming from my eyes, I went to get it to see who'd called me. Three voicemails and eighteen missed calls? My mum must have been frantic. Listening to two voicemails confirmed it. Both times, she begged me to call her as soon as possible, and I could just imagine her trying to keep herself busy while she waited for the phone to ring.

I'm a bad daughter.

I should have phoned her right after I left the hospital but I couldn't think clearly enough to hold a conversation. Sleep helped a little, but I still wasn't ready to hear the sadness in her voice over my split with Drew.

To avoid it for a bit longer, I listened to the final message on my answer phone, sure it would be Mum again.

Wrong.

"Hello, Ellie. This is Jayne Black. I didn't want to do this over voicemail, but I've been trying to get through all day. The thing is, Ellie, while I love your work and think you'd be perfect for the job, I'm afraid after seeing today's newspapers, I have to take back my offer. *'Where Are You, Grey Rabbit?'* is a children's book, and while I don't know the ins and outs of your life, your name is now associated with drugs, and I can't afford to have anyone who might damage my reputation working with me. I really am sorry to do this to you. I'd be more than happy to provide you with a glowing reference if you ever need one, but that's all I can offer now. If you'd like to discuss this further, please call me. And again, I'm so sorry."

My phone dropped from my hand, and a bitter laugh echoed through the room. Derek had called the publicity "an opportunity." Instead, I'd lost the one job I'd always wanted. I'd lost everything I'd ever wanted. I couldn't find anywhere to lay the blame. Was it Jason's fault for outing my relationship with Drew so the reporters found out my name? Or for taking drugs and creating the story that got me fired? Was Drew to blame because, if he wasn't so stubborn and angry, maybe Jason wouldn't have used? Was it my fault for trying to protect Drew and having it all backfire?

It didn't fall on one single person. Between the three of us, we'd created this mess, and how did it end up? One in hospital, one fired, and one thinking he'd always be second best.

All three of us miserable and alone.

Calling Mum would have to wait. I folded my legs underneath me, grabbed a sofa cushion to hold on to, and gently rocked myself back and forth as silent tears fell from my eyes.

It didn't take long for the events of the past few days to sweep through my friends and family. Only those closest to me knew the whole truth, at least in regards to Drew, and my firing. It was hard to appreciate the concerned phone calls when I wanted to be left alone to come to terms with everything. The press weren't given any official word on my break up with Drew, but he was photographed looking miserable, and since I hadn't been seen with him, they reached their own conclusions. The bonus of having very few close friends was that there was nobody to sell the real story.

Jason wasn't getting as much of a hard time as I'd expected with the press or the public, mainly thanks to Derek's quick thinking and super media skills. He didn't try to cover up the overdose. Instead, he pushed the seriousness of Jason's "condition" in a bid to gain sympathy. It worked spectacularly, and Razes Hell's return to the music scene was already being hotly anticipated. I'd never put much faith in Derek as anything more than a greedy chancer, but he'd come through for all of us when things got rough. For the first time ever, I was glad we had him on our side.

The sting of losing my illustrating job wouldn't wear off no matter how hard I tried to distract myself. I didn't call Jayne Black after the message she left. What would I say? *Thanks for being so polite when you fired me?* I knew the only words out of my mouth would be grovelly ones and she'd obviously made up her mind, so I let it go and holed myself up in my workroom, waiting for inspiration. Even that depressed me. The "vase" Drew and I attempted still sat at my potter's wheel. Deformed as it was, I couldn't bring myself to throw it out.

I'd reached *that* level of lame.

Life without Drew was weird. Even before we got together, it was unusual for more than a couple of days to pass without us having some kind of contact. Time away from him after being completely wrapped up in each other was torture. Every muscle in my body ached with missing him; misery had settled into my bones, pressing into my flesh and making every movement painful.

So I didn't move.

I'd reached for the phone a million times to call Drew. I never dialled because ultimately, I knew what I'd get. Deflected to voicemail, or yelled at to leave him alone. I didn't need further confirmation of how badly I'd hurt him, and if he answered, hearing the pain in his voice would have killed me.

I couldn't visit Jason because he wasn't allowed visitors for the first week of rehab. Being cut off from both of my favourite people in the world was like living without oxygen. I struggled to breathe, to function properly, always aware a fundamental part of life – my life – was missing.

The evening before I was allowed to see Jason, my sister showed up at my flat holding two boxes of pizza, and a bag filled with alcopops. She declared it was girls' night, and set up the food and drinks on the coffee table before I could protest.

"Don't you have college in the morning?" I asked, as Lucy rifled through the kitchen drawer.

"I do, but I'm willing to blow it off in the name of a hangover." She emerged triumphant from the kitchen, bottle opener in hand. "Let's get this party started!"

"We're not having a party, Lucy," I groaned, falling backwards onto the sofa and tucking my hands inside the sleeves of my oversized jumper.

"Okay, not a party. But we're not sitting in your workroom, staring at your paints and a blank canvas, either. We're going to eat junk food, drink alcohol, and chat the way sisters are supposed to now I'm old enough to get smashed."

The corners of my mouth twitched. Leave it to Lucy to attempt to pull me out of my funk. The girl was an unstoppable force of happy.

"Okay, *baby sister.*" I sat up a bit and flipped open the lid of one of the pizza boxes. *Mmm, meat feast.* "But not too much drinking, okay?"

She grinned. "We'll see!"

Two hours later, both pizzas were gone, along with eight bottles of Smirnoff Ice.

I'd never been much of a drinker, so the three and a half bottles I consumed quickly went to my head. Luckily, Lucy and I were both happy drunks, and as we sprawled across the living room floor, stuffed with food, life didn't seem quite so bad.

"I suppose you want to stay here tonight?"

"I have to. Mum and Dad will kill you if I return home in this state!"

"Hey, you were the one who brought the booze!"

"And as a responsible older sibling, you should have limited me to one bottle." She giggled, and patted her stomach. "You probably should have stopped me eating after the first half pizza, too."

"Oh, please. There's nothing of you!"

Nobody ever believed we were sisters, since she was a perfect size eight, with long legs and not an extra ounce of fat on her. Me? I'd learned to love my curves years ago.

"You should make the most of your figure," I teased. "It won't last forever!"

"I bloody hope not, I want some boobs one day."

I snorted out a laugh. "You're gorgeous as you are, Luce."

"Easy for you to say with your massive hooters!"

"They're not massive." I laughed, throwing a cushion across the room at her. "They're... well proportioned."

"Whatever. I want some. Boys like boobs."

She let out a sigh, casting a shadow over the light conversation, and I sat up a little. So much for us being happy drunks.

"Luce? What's going on with you? The other night you said you weren't interested in boys."

"I'm not." She paused, fiddling with the embroidery on the cushion. "Well. No. I'm not, it's... what were you doing when you were eighteen?"

"What do you mean? Are you asking if I had a boyfriend?"

She shrugged. "I guess. I'm eighteen years old and I've never been kissed."

Wow. I never thought my first big sister talk would happen under the influence of alcohol. Maybe that was why she felt brave enough to ask. It's not that we weren't close. We just weren't secret-sharing close. This was brand new territory.

"Well," I propped myself against the sofa, preparing to sound all wise and profound, "I didn't have my first kiss until my eighteenth birthday."

"So... you had a boyfriend when you were eighteen?"

"Not exactly. I didn't have a proper boyfriend until I was at university."

Lucy straightened up a little, smirking as if she was about to land a major scoop. "Does this mean the kiss on your birthday was a crafty one with a stranger?"

Oh boy.

"No. It wasn't a one-off or a stranger."

"But it wasn't a boyfriend?"

"It was Jason."

The smirk slipped from Lucy's face as her jaw dropped. "Jason? *Jason?* Your first kiss was with Jason Brooks?"

I nodded and took a small sip of my drink while she processed the information. Every time I blinked, her expression switched, from shock, to confusion, to wide-eyed disbelief, until settling on how-the-hell-did-that-ever-happen?

"I had a gigantic crush on him when I was growing up," I explained. "I didn't know if he knew, or if he cared, or if he only saw me as a friend. Do you remember Mum and Dad taking you to Grandma's the weekend of my eighteenth so I could have a party?"

Lucy nodded. "I hated you because you wouldn't let me stay."

"Yeah, you did." I laughed. "Well, I was really surprised when Jason and Drew showed up because I didn't think they'd want to hang out with my friends, but they did. They were the last ones to leave. Jason gave me my first kiss when he said goodnight."

Eighteen seemed a million years ago, and that night felt like another life. In many ways, it was.

Lucy was silent for a few minutes. "What was it like?"

"Well, first kisses are always-"

"No," she interrupted. "What was it like kissing Jason?"

Her cheeks flamed and she closed her eyes, burying her face into the cushion I'd thrown at her.

What the hell?

"Wh...? Lucy, are you... do you...?"

"Yes," she mumbled from behind her cushion-shield. "I like Jason."

I sat bolt upright. "*Jason?*"

I must be more pissed than I thought. Lucy. Jason? Too insane for words.

"What?" Lucy asked. "You liked him once, too."

"Well, yes. But... it's not the same thing. You... I... why?"

"Why do you think? He's Jason Brooks. I like him for the same reasons a million other girls do."

I shook my head. "I'm not buying it. Other girls are into him because he's famous and he knows how to rock the stage. You know him for real."

Well. Kind of. At least, she knew he was more than his onstage persona.

"I like that, too. How he's real, and although he becomes someone else on stage, he's still mostly himself. He's funny and honest and... gorgeous." Her face flushed brighter and she pulled the cushion closer to her. "Anyway, it's no big deal."

"If you didn't think it was a big deal, you wouldn't be hiding."

"He's your best friend and you're my sister. It's embarrassing. More so now I've discovered you used to go out with him!"

"I didn't go out with him. We got drunk a few times and... stuff happened."

She winced as if my words caused her actual, physical pain. "What kind of stuff? Oh my God, did you have sex with him?"

"No! Mostly kissing. We were young, we drank a lot, and we ended up in my room at uni and there was... occasional... touching. But nothing heavy!" I added, quickly. "Drunken fumbling before we passed out."

"Did you want to have sex with him?"

"Lucy, come on!" I stood up and busied myself collecting the empty bottles. "Why are you grilling me about something that happened six years ago?"

I desperately regretted telling her the truth, but how was I to know she was harbouring a crush? I cast my mind back, looking for signs. The other night at my parents' house, she blushed a few times when he talked to her, but... she could be shy sometimes, even around people she knew. I remembered how she wiggled her hips and eyebrows when she asked him if he wanted to join in with the dance game, but she was on a total high from the fame she'd get from me dating Drew. What about before then? Christmas? Jason got drunk after Christmas dinner and fell asleep on the sofa and she covered him with a blanket. Wouldn't anyone do that, though?

"I want to know."

Oh, wow. She's got it bad.

With a sigh, I put the bottles back on the table and sank down to the floor beside her.

"I thought I wanted to be with him but he didn't want a relationship, he wanted to screw around. I didn't want that kind of relationship with him. Or anyone. Then I met someone else and it was all over."

"Just like that?"

I nodded. "It was nothing more than two drunken idiots messing around."

"Didn't it hurt to let him go?"

"No. He was still my best friend. All I let go of was a silly, childish crush."

"Is that what I have? A crush?"

"I don't know." I pulled her into a one-armed hug. "Does it feel like a crush?"

Lucy shrugged again, and rested her head on my shoulder. "I suppose that's all it'll ever be. To him, I'm just your little sister."

"Well, he *is* ten years older than you."

"Drew's eight years older than you. Ten isn't much more of a difference."

It's a big difference when you're eighteen.

The mention of Drew's name punctured through my comfortable, tipsy fog, and stabbed at my chest. "Drew used to think I was 'just Jason's childish friend.' I'm pretty sure he thinks that now, too."

Lucy snuggled in closer to me, resting her hand on mine. "Sorry, Ellie. I didn't mean to bring him up tonight. I'm supposed to be cheering you up. Instead, I'm whining that Jason – who has way bigger issues right now – doesn't know I'm alive."

Eight years, ten years. It wasn't such a big deal, except Jason was currently in rehab for cocaine addiction. I wasn't sure how I felt about my sister having any kind of feelings for him. A little too weird to comprehend. No doubt he saw Lucy was a stunner, but I figured she was right. He didn't think of her *that* way. I hoped for her sake it was nothing more than a passing phase. If I'd learned anything over the course of my life, it was that mixing lifelong friendships with romance could get complicated *really* fast.

chapter sixteen
Like A T-Rex With An Ice Cream Headache

"Ellie, you insensitive bint," Jason whispered in my ear as he pulled me into a hug. "Walking into a rehabilitation centre with a hangover? You should be ashamed of yourself!"

He chuckled as I hugged him back.

"Urgh," I groaned. "Busted."

My super slow walk with lowered head probably gave me away. I'd put on a little extra make-up too, to cover up my pale cheeks. Actually, *that* was probably the giveaway.

He was absolutely right. I had no business parading last night's drunkenness in front of a room full of addicts. I'd woken up, groaning like a T-Rex with an ice cream headache, and Lucy was in an equally bad way. I probably should have felt bad about letting her get so drunk, but - mutual misery aside – we'd had a fun evening.

"How are you doing?" I asked.

"Not too bad," Jason answered as we strolled across the common room to a vacant sofa. "The cravings vary from day to day, or hour to hour, but it's under control. It helps that this place is a lot nicer than the last one."

I glanced around the room, taking in the soothing, pale blue walls hung with seascapes, and the modern furniture; cosy and adorned with squishy cushions. Definitely an improvement. Jason's previous rehabilitation centre had the vibe of a nursing home; all floral patterns and frills.

Jason certainly looked better than he did the last time I saw him. His face had more colour, but the dark circles under his eyes and the stiffness of his movements showed me he wasn't feeling as well as he pretended to be. How could he be? Withdrawal was hard on its own, but throw in a crumbling family, guilt, and pressure to get back on his feet for the band, and it was obvious he'd be struggling with it all.

As Jason's eyes met mine, he wrapped his arm around my shoulders. My delicate physical condition combined with my less than perfect mental state made me fall against him, teary-eyed.

Familiarity. That was what I needed. Jason's hugs were about the most familiar thing in the world to me, more so than hugs from my family. It was kind of nostalgic. Like rediscovering the favourite childhood toy I used to reach for when I had a nightmare. Perhaps it should have been awkward. Or I should have felt like a traitor for visiting Jason but not calling Drew. Or maybe I was supposed to still be angry with Jason for landing himself back in rehab. Instead, I felt relieved. Relieved to be with someone who didn't need an instruction manual for my brain.

And I knew it was what he needed, too.

"I missed you. I know that's selfish since you've been stuck in here trying to deal with stuff but... I missed you."

"You're not selfish. If anyone's selfish, it's me. I'm in here, safe. I left you out in the real world dealing with all my mess."

"This is where you need to be. Although, I sort of wish I could hide, too."

Jason smiled. "If the staff realise how hungover you are, they might make a bed up for you!"

"Shut up." I smacked his arm as I sat up, blinking the moisture from my eyes. "Tell me how you really are, Jason."

He paused for a second, as if considering whether or not to tell me the truth. "I've been better. I should have phoned you the night before I came here but I didn't ... I wasn't sure if you wanted to talk to me." He lowered his gaze, and shuffled a little in his seat. "I know we were okay when you left the hospital. I didn't know if we'd still be okay once you'd had time to think."

Time to think was all I'd had. Thoughts kept me awake, stilted my concentration for even the smallest tasks, and made me hurt in ways I never knew were possible. I'd never felt anything other than sadness for Jason. Well, aside from the guilt because I hadn't realised what he'd been going through.

"We're okay," I told him. "I'm sorry I didn't come back to see you, it was just... being back in the hospital was the worst place to be. I didn't want to fight through the journalists, I didn't know how much people knew about what I did-"

"Ellie, wait." Jason held up his hands. "I know you think you did a horrible thing by lying for me-"

"It *was* horrible. I could have killed you."

"No, *I* could have killed me. I was an asshole for asking you to lie for me. I should have let you do what you wanted to do. What you said in the hospital was right. Either way, I was going to end up in rehab. I didn't know how much I needed to be here until I sat in my old bedroom, lining up the coke in front of me. It was too late for me to stop when I'd got that far. I should have called you to help me but the cocaine took over." He paused, shaking his head. "I can't explain it any better."

We'd been through this so many times. Jason trying to explain why he did what he did, and me trying hard to make sense of his reasons, but failing because I'd never been an addict. There's only so far understanding can go when you've never been in another person's position. Battling so hard, and stumbling every time because that thing, that hook they needed to keep them going kept calling out, tempting them back.

"I'm scared, Ellie. I'm scared no matter how hard I try, I'm always going to end up here."

Jason threw his head back, and I covered his hand with mine, gripping tightly as if my hold could save him, drag him back from his fears. "Hey," I said trying to control my shaky voice. "I don't want to hear you talk that way. You managed two years clean at a time when you couldn't get out of bed without using. You're more determined now. I saw it in your eyes when you were in hospital."

"Do you see it now?" he asked, the last of his bravado slipping away.

I gave a weak smile as a tear dripped down my cheek. "Yeah. I do. Buried deep, but it's there."

"I can't feel it."

"You will. As long as you don't stop looking."

Jason released my hand and pulled me into another hug, clinging to me. I hugged him back equally as hard, our tears raining down on each other. I didn't care about the other people in the room. Chances were, they'd all had a similar conversation with their own friends and family, and although it would have been better in private, what mattered was Jason's honesty. Keeping everything bottled up was how he, and all of us, landed up in such a mess. The only way through was by opening up.

"How's the counselling going?" I asked, eager to move on to a less soul-crushing conversation.

"It's good. I don't feel like I'm talking to a counsellor, it's more like I'm having a chat with someone who knows what I've been through. Well, I *am*. A few of the workers here trained to do this job *because* they've been in my position."

"What do you talk about? I mean, you don't have to tell me-"

"Mostly Drew."

Aaand, back to soul-crushing.

"Have you seen him?"

Jason shook his head. "Not since I was in hospital. Dad said Drew waited around until he arrived, but I didn't see him after he stormed out."

That was Drew. Although he didn't want to talk to his brother, he still refused to leave him alone at the hospital. He cared enough to wait, in spite of his own pain.

A familiar ache pushed at my insides. I missed his face, his smile, the feel of his hand in mine, his hands on me.

Everything.

"One of the reasons we're not allowed visitors for the first week in here is so we have time to think. And no matter how much you're going to tell me what happened between you and Drew isn't my fault, I know it is."

I opened my mouth to speak, but Jason continued. "It's not only about you and Drew. Dad told me about your illustrating job. I'm gonna... when I get out of here, I'll do all I can to help you. If I hadn't ended up in hospital, you wouldn't have gotten fired. I need to fix it."

"You can't fix it. I'd probably have lost the job anyway once the author realised I was dating a member of a rock band, and you can't fix me and Drew because he doesn't want us fixed. I lied to him. I did everything he was worried I'd do. How can I expect him to trust me?"

"I'm not having that." Jason shook his head. "Why are you giving up?"

"Don't make it sound as if I don't care. I know how his mind works and no amount of talking will take back what I did. You of all people should understand how hard he clings onto the things that hurt him."

"If you give up on him, you'll hurt him more."

"I'm scared, okay? I hate being away from him, it's killing me. But I can't win him back with a few sweet words, and I can't try because I don't ever want to hear him tell me it's over again. I can't do it."

I'd relived the moment Drew walked away from me so many times, and it never hurt any less to visualise the look on his face before he said his last words to me. At the time, I couldn't imagine hurting any more. Each day, I was proved wrong. Regular visits from my parents didn't do much to lift my mood. They came, forced me to eat, tried to make me call Drew, then left. I'd expected Jason to understand my reasons for not talking to Drew, even if my mum and dad didn't.

"Ellie. If you let this go, you'll regret it. I saw how you were together and how much he needed you when he was arguing with me, and I'm a dick for not seeing it before. Because it's been obvious for a long time. He's completely in love with you, and that isn't going to change overnight."

I closed my eyes, the ache taking over, colliding with my hangover and ripping through me so I folded in half, resting my forehead on Jason's knees.

chapter seventeen
Nobody Knows

I wasn't sure if it was my raging hangover or the emotion I cried out with Jason, but every part of my body hurt. It took days to recover, and I spent all of them thinking about the things Jason had said. I loved that he wanted to help me, I just couldn't see any way he could. There was no "fix" for Drew and me. I could have apologised again. I could have waited outside his window and grovelled, and I would have if I thought it would make a difference. The fact remained, I'd broken his trust and he'd closed off from me as though we never existed. I didn't know how to fight that.

At some point, I knew I'd have to get back to normality, so I dragged my miserable arse out of my flat and headed out to visit my parents. I hadn't been to their house since the night Jason overdosed; hadn't been anywhere other than the supermarket and the rehab centre. I figured Mum and Dad would be glad to see me wearing proper clothes instead of pyjamas or trackie bottoms and a hoodie, until I realised that at eleven a.m on a weekday, they probably wouldn't be in.

As I pulled up outside my family home, I did a quick scan around for Drew's car, just in case by some weird coincidence, he was visiting his dad. All clear.

Great. Now what?

"Ellie!"

Lucy must have seen my car through the window. She stood on the doorstep, beaming, bouncing on the balls of her feet.

Sheesh, she needs to ease off the coffee.

"Morning, Luce." I climbed out of the car, my bag slung over my shoulder.

"I'm so glad you're here!"

"What's up?"

Lucy ran down the path, her fingers digging into my arm as she pulled me into the living room and sat me in my dad's armchair - a strong indication he definitely wasn't home.

"Wait there," Lucy said, before skipping out and thundering up the stairs.

Okay. My sister had always been sunny, but the way she darted around the house, all smiley and secretive was downright creepy. She'd hardly spoken a word, yet she appeared giddy with barely contained glee. I felt as though I'd slipped into the start of a horror movie, where the person who looked like Lucy was actually some alien life form from another planet on a mission to take over the world, one human at a time.

When she returned, she had her hands behind her back.

"Seriously. What's going on?"

"I'm about to tell you, dear sister." She paused to giggle. "Okay, I have a gift for you, but you can't look until I've gone. I need to take a shower, and when I come back, we'll talk."

My immediate thought was she had a pregnancy test gripped in her hands, and needed the time to shower for me to calm down enough not to strangle her. Based on our conversation a few nights ago, I knew I was letting my mind run away with me. Besides, she was way too happy for that to be the case.

"What is it?" I asked, a hint of nervousness creeping into my voice.

"It's nothing bad. It's... an idea. From Jason."

"Wait. How have you been getting *ideas* from Jason?"

Her words came out in a rush. "I went to visit him yesterday. I booked an appointment because... I wanted to see him."

Any hope I'd had that her feelings for Jason were a passing phase vanished when my brain registered the look on her face. Somewhere between happiness at seeing him and sadness... maybe because he showed no sign of thinking of her as anything more than a little sister.

"How is he?" I hoped to distract her with facts, rather than allowing her mind to wander.

"Determined. He's determined to get out of that place and not go back. And," she added, her smile returning, "he's determined to help you."

Yup. That was Jason. Once he got an idea, he wouldn't let go until every possibility of it working out had been blasted to pieces. I appreciated his efforts, I just didn't think there was any plan he could concoct that had a shot at succeeding. And involving Lucy? This wasn't her battle to fight, and if she mistook his trust to help with this for more, she would get hurt.

I didn't have the strength to hold both of us together.

"I'm going to visit him tomorrow," I said. "Couldn't it have waited until then?"

"Probably. But he gave me the... *idea*, hoping you'll have made a decision by the time you see him."

"Fine. What is it?"

Lucy released her hands from behind her back and handed me an A4 sized padded envelope. The contents were super thin because I couldn't feel anything through the inner bubble wrap.

"You have to read the letter carefully, and think before you say no. Jason said you're going to refuse, and asked me to tell you it's not as crazy as it seems." She stared at me, as if the fate of the whole universe was in my hands. "Okay. I'll let you read in peace."

Once she left the room, the only sound was my deep breathing as I tried to work out what might be in the envelope, and why Jason was so sure I'd refuse.

Wait. What was I thinking? If it was Jason's idea, it would probably be insane, so of course I'd reject it. On the other hand... Jason's crazy ideas often worked out.

"Oh bloody hell," I muttered, tearing into the package and upturning it so the contents spilled into my lap.

Two pieces of writing paper and a CD.

Okay.

I picked up the piece of paper that fell out first, and my breath hitched as I read:

Nobody Knows lyrics by Drew Brooks

A little girl, a lonely step
A little boy who didn't know who he was yet
She held his hand, she dried his tears
Picking up the fragments of shattered years

Asking nothing, she waited there
With a patient smile and cranberry-scented hair
I needed her, my light, my sun
I never knew what she'd become

Nobody knows how hard I tried
To fix the pain buried inside
To keep on swimming when I wanted to drown
To stop the waves from pulling me down
Nobody knows how much it takes
To stay complete when I want to break
When there's nothing left one thing is true
Nobody knows but you

Tears blurred my vision so I couldn't read anymore, but Drew's familiar scrawl and his beautiful words hit me deep in my chest. My song. The song he'd hidden from me in London. I could never have imagined such perfect lyrics. Lyrics that reflected everything we'd been through from the start. All this time, he remembered the day we met, the way I sat quietly beside him and waited for him to be ready to play. The way I *always* waited for him.

How much more amazing would it have been if Drew had shown me the song? I'd have hugged him so hard. Told him how much it meant that he'd written words I felt in every part of me. They *were* a part of me. Part of us.

A tear dripped onto the page and I quickly moved the paper aside so as not to smudge the words.

God, I miss him so much.

To distract myself from the feeling of my insides shrivelling, I picked up the other piece of paper.

This is the one song for the new album Drew kept from me. He didn't want me, or anyone to see until everyone knew you were together. He gave it to Mack, and he still wants it on the album, even though it's so different from what we normally do, but he won't play it live.

Mack recorded a version of the song on the CD enclosed. It's only him and a guitar, and it's fucking brilliant. You wanna get Drew back? Learn it. Derek has arranged a small homecoming gig for us in three weeks, when I'm out of rehab. It'll be invite only, family and friends, and some people from town who have always supported us. Sing the song. Tweak the lyrics and sing it for him, Ellie. You can do this.

Think about it.

Jason

Sing the song. Sing the song? *He must still be high.*

Did he not know Drew at all? How could I get up in front of the people we knew best and sing a song he himself didn't want to sing? Being the centre of attention was not Drew's thing. That was why he liked the drums so much. He could do what he loved while hiding at the back of the stage. If I made some massive deal about this song...

I couldn't see how it would help.

With a sigh, I picked up the CD, twirling it around in my fingers. Part of me felt hearing those lyrics come to life would be peering into a part of Drew's brain he didn't want me to see. *He still wants it on the album. Soon, everyone will see.*

A ripple of hope trickled through me. If he didn't want me to hear the song, why would he want it recorded? A permanent record of his feelings would surely be the last thing he'd want if he was done with me.

Unless... he wanted to remind me what I threw away.

I rose from my seat and removed Mum's Olly Murs album from the CD player, replacing it with Jason's gift.

My heart stilled as the gentle strains of Mack's guitar played through the speakers. Although the melody was soft, it still somehow had a little of their signature darkness. I couldn't help imagining how cool it would sound with the addition of drums to make it heavier.

It really was beautiful.

"So, what do you think?"

I jumped at the sound of Lucy's voice. She stood behind me, eyebrows raised. The hopefulness of her expression was both frustrating and amusing.

"Have you heard this?" I nodded towards the CD player.

"No. Jason told me I couldn't see or hear until you did."

"The lyrics are on the chair. Take a look."

As Lucy scanned the words, a smile formed on her lips.

"You're so lucky. This is fab! He wrote a song for you. I would love it if a guy did that for me."

"Except he's not *my* guy anymore."

Lucy glanced at me over the top of the lyric sheet. "He could be if you do what Jason wants you to do."

I sank to the floor. "It's a terrible idea."

"Why? Is there anything more romantic than someone you love singing for you? Come on, Ellie. They might be Drew's lyrics but they fit you, too. You know what he's trying to say here, and I know you feel the same way. He's the one. The only one who knows everything about you."

Yup. It was true, he was the one. It still sometimes astounded me how we hadn't always been so close, but knowing each other forever made it easy for us to see how much sense we made. Jason and I could communicate without speaking, but he didn't speak to my heart the way Drew did.

Drew was everything.

"I wish it was easy, Lucy. I wish I could say Jason's idea is total genius but it's not that simple. First of all, remember what happened last time I got on stage?"

I shuddered, thinking about all those eyes on me, and me freezing up then running away. It made me sick to imagine getting on a stage again and attempting to sing. If I couldn't sing a cover of a song I knew inside out with my best friend, how would I be able to overcome the emotion of a song that meant so much? That had so much resting on it?

A sudden desperate need to be alone forced me to my feet, and I picked up the lyric sheet, Jason's letter and the CD, and stuffed them into my bag.

"Ellie, what are you doing?"

"I need to go home." Claustrophobia bore down on me the way it did at the hospital. "Thank you for passing the message on, but I need to think."

I rushed out the front door, and started down the path, halting abruptly as I spotted Drew getting out of his car.

Drew. For the first time since we broke up.

For the briefest second, his eyes brightened. The light faded as quickly as it appeared though, and everything inside me dissolved, emptying me of the last of my hope.

But he didn't make any move to leave. Swallowing down the lump in my throat, I tried to speak.

"I... It's... Hi."

"Hi."

Okay, he didn't tell you to get lost. Let's try for something resembling English this time.

"How are you?"

Ooh, aren't we Wordy Worderson today? The feeling of wanting to leap into his arms rushed over me, but I knew he wouldn't catch me. Wouldn't let me cuddle into his chest. Wouldn't let me breathe in his scent, and feel as special as I always felt when I was wrapped up in him. And I knew it because he folded his arms across his chest to keep a barrier between us. There was already a reasonable sized garden separating us. I'd hurt him badly enough that - clearly - he felt he needed some extra protection.

"I'm okay. How are you?"

"I'm... okay."

I'm not okay.

"I've just come over to take Dad to see Jason."

My eyebrows shot upwards. "Are you going to see him too?"

Drew shook his head, his eyes expressionless and my heart sank. It was probably still too soon for him, but for a second I'd thought maybe... maybe he was ready.

My legs wanted to bolt away, to end the awkwardness. I couldn't stand how much I wanted, *needed*, to touch him, and if I stayed any longer, I'd crumble. Fall at his feet, and have to deal with the rejection I'd promised myself I wouldn't go through again.

Nobody knows how much it takes to stay complete when I want to break. When there's nothing left one thing is true. Nobody knows but you.

My knees buckled as the words drifted through my mind, as clear as if someone had hooked up an iPod directly to my brain. Drew didn't know I'd heard his lyrics, but when his eyes met mine, I felt sure he was thinking about them, too.

"Ellie, I... I have to go."

I nodded. He threw me a sad smile, a smile which both warmed me and broke my heart at the same time. It was *the* smile. The one he reserved only for me. Just... an unhappier version.

"See ya," I said, fighting the sting of hot tears behind my eyes.

"See ya."

Drew continued on his way to his dad's house, and I quickly clambered into my car, throwing my bag down on the passenger seat.

It wasn't the easiest conversation we'd ever had - it was barely a conversation - but it was the one that needed to happen. The first one after the break-up. I never expected him to magically forgive me for stomping on his heart, on his trust. It was pretty amazing he managed to stay around me for longer than a minute before making an excuse to get away.

And that smile. That was the part I clung to, because maybe it meant we could re-build what we had. Maybe it meant, although he hated it, he understood what I did.

Or maybe I was deluding myself out of desperation. Life without him was like living inside a black and white television. Everything still worked as normal, but the brightness was missing. My world was dull, lacking in clarity.

Was Jason right? Was it all down to me to make this better? Could I get up in front of a crowd and make Drew understand how much I loved him?

There were so many ways Jason's plan could go wrong. Only one way it could go right. Best case scenario, I'd get the happy ending. Worst case scenario, I'd get through the song, only for Drew to tell me how awful I am, leaving me alone on the stage while the audience stared at me with pitying eyes, muttering how bad they felt for me. Or sniggering at me for being so stupid.

In spite of the hideous realisation I might be completely humiliated, there was a voice in my head, a feeling in my gut telling me Jason had provided me with everything I needed to get Drew back.

I wasn't sure if I had the strength.

chapter eighteen

"Ellie, are you sure you've really thought about this?"

Jason's eyes bore into me like laser beams, cutting through me, searching for the truth.

Again, we sat in the rehab centre's common room as people came and went around us, some of them with their own visitors, some just sitting quietly, staring into space. This was only my second visit but it was already familiar enough to feel comfortable, more like a cool hangout spot than what it really was.

"I haven't thought about anything else. I didn't sleep, I couldn't work. I can't get that song out of my head, Jason. But I can't sing it. I can't."

"And I thought Lucy could persuade you to do anything."

"Yeah, about that," I sat up straighter. "Why did you get her involved in this? It's bad enough dealing with you nagging me."

Lucy's interest in Jason was the other thing that kept me awake. It wasn't my place to tell her who she could or couldn't be friends with; I was her sister, not her mother. I couldn't stop worrying she might mistake Jason's intentions towards her, though. She wanted a way to get closer to him, and he'd given it to her with no idea what effect it would have.

"Lucy's worried about you." Jason said. "She told me she wished she could help so I–"

"You turned her into your delivery girl."

"Stop making it sound so sneaky. She came here, she wanted to do something for you so I asked her to give you the CD. I didn't lure her here with cookies and chocolate. She came to me."

You wouldn't need to lure her. Just ask, and she'll come running.

"Be careful with her, please," I said. "I don't want her getting mixed up in anything that might backfire on her."

"Such as? She passed on a message, that's all."

The words, '*she's got a crush on you, okay?*' were halfway up my throat before I swallowed them back. I couldn't do that to her, even if it made Jason understand why he had to be careful. It'd be way too embarrassing for her, and she'd never forgive me.

"Whatever," I said. "I just don't want her worrying about me and Drew when she should be focusing on college."

"Okay. Message received. No more errand running for Lucy. *I'm* not done with you, though."

"Yeah, well we've been through this, and I told you. I need some time."

"I'm giving you three weeks."

"And what happens if I put myself out there and he rejects me? Again. There'll be people with cameras, just like last time. I don't want that moment plastered all over the Internet. I've had enough of my private moments finding their way to entertainment websites. The last one led to me losing my dream job, remember?"

Jason's face fell, and it made me feel like a bitch because I wasn't trying to remind him of his part in it. I just needed him to understand why I wasn't ready to lay everything on the line.

"Jason, can't you try to see where I'm coming from? I know you want to help me, I do."

"So let me. Mack said he'll come by your place so you can try it out with the guitar, and just... just try."

I rolled my eyes. "You really have all the answers, don't you?"

"Yes. I do." He smiled, and for the first time in forever a little sparkle flickered in his eyes. Relieved as I was to see it, it appeared for the wrong reason. He couldn't force me to do something that terrified me to the point of nausea.

"Ellie-" he stopped abruptly, focusing on a point over my shoulder, his eyebrows pulling together in confusion. I twisted around, and my breath hitched.

Through the glass doors at the far end of the room, Drew was talking to a member of staff.

Drew. I'd avoided him since the hospital, and now I'd seen him two days in a row.

Even from a distance, my body reacted. My pulse raced with the need to run to him and launch myself into his arms. Since that wasn't an option, I turned back to Jason. "Were you expecting him today?"

Jason shook his head. "I've no idea why he's here."

I flicked my head towards the doors again, hoping to gauge what was happening but I was too far away to tell. Drew nodded to the guy he was talking to, his face serious, and when he turned to leave, his gaze fell on me. For the briefest second, his eyes brightened. The light faded as quickly as it appeared and after a few moments he walked away without looking back.

Everything inside me dissolved, emptying me of the last of my hope, but at the same time, something else rose inside me and I sprang to my feet.

My body and my brain disconnected as I ran across the room, through the glass doors to the reception area, then outside.

"Drew!"

He'd just reached his car and he stopped, turning at the sound of my voice. He stared at me expectantly. I couldn't read anything else in his face. His eyes didn't flicker with happiness this time. They just stared at me, waiting. He'd already put up his protective barriers so he wouldn't have to deal with his feelings. The emptiness in his eyes was familiar. He'd gone to that place in his mind where emotions didn't exist. I always hated that; the way he slipped into denial. But in that moment, standing so close to him and knowing I couldn't go to him and help him open up, I wished I could do the same.

My brain jolted back to life and I realised I had absolutely no idea why I'd sprinted out to him. No explanation for me speeding through the rehab centre like Superman on a mission to rescue someone from danger.

Maybe it was me I was trying to rescue. Or Drew. To stop him getting wound up about me visiting Jason. Whatever. I'd sprinted in a way that would have made Mo Farah proud, so I had to say something.

"I'm here because Dad asked me to visit Jason," Drew said. "I don't want to be here."

He didn't need to add the last comment, his feelings were clear. Well, his *I'm a hardass* alter ego was clear. That wasn't Drew talking. Not really.

"You should stay, Drew. I'm nearly finished, anyway."

"What's the point? I have nothing to say to him."

"So why did you come?"

"I told you. Dad wanted me to-"

I shook my head, halting him. Had he really forgotten already that I could see through any lie he attempted to tell me? That I knew him better than anyone? That after a few seconds of really focusing on his eyes I wouldn't see the pain inside them? Inside him.

"What does it matter?" he asked. "I'm here, and surprise surprise, you beat me to it."

His tone was like a sucker punch to my gut. I wanted to scream. Why didn't he understand that I hurt too? That being around Jason was a lifeline. He was my friend, I wanted to be there for him, but part of me visiting him was about me scrabbling around, trying to cling onto what was left of my life before the band, before the publicity, before my world exploded and crumbled at my feet.

But screaming would do no good. Drew had built up his barriers to keep me out and that made it so much easier for him to lash out at me. To say things he knew deep down were unfair.

Blinking back tears I breathed deeply, building my own barriers up again.

Drew scrubbed his hands over his face, his hand reaching for me then stopping and falling to his side again. "Ells."

"I have to go."

What else could I do? I wanted him back. God, I wanted him back so much. He wasn't ready to hear me. Wasn't ready to let me try.

As I walked away from him, the fractured remains of my heart shattered, yet just as I'd held on to the smile he gave me the day before, I grasped onto the brightness in his eyes when he saw me. Gathered it in tight because I needed something. Something to let me know he still cared.

chapter nineteen

Best Friends Forever

Over the next three weeks, many things happened:

- I took a leap of faith, and told Jason I would sing Drew's song.
- Mack came to my flat twice a week to help me learn *Nobody Knows*, and practice with his guitar.
- Lucy was so excited I'd agreed to Jason's plan, she called me every two days to check I was still going through with it.
- Jason spent my visiting time with him telling me everything would be fine, and making sure all was in place for my performance to go smoothly.
- Drew started going to counselling sessions at the rehab centre to help him and Jason try to work through their problems.

That was my favourite part of the weeks leading up to my big performance. According to Jason, Drew wasn't entirely happy about going to therapy, but he cared enough to try, and after everything, I was proud of him for making the effort.

It was Drew's strength that helped me reach my decision about singing for him. If he could push through the pain to get his relationship with Jason back on track, I could battle my nerves to show him how much he meant to me. I *would*. Being apart from Drew didn't get any easier. In fact, every day of those three weeks seemed to drag me down more. Having something to work towards was the only thing keeping me going when all I wanted was to hole myself up in my room and torment myself for the mistakes I made. I needed Drew to know how sorry I was, and maybe take away some of the misery I knew he felt. Whatever happened afterwards, he had to know I was sorry.

The night of Razes Hell's comeback gig was hotly anticipated around town. It wasn't exactly a homecoming because they'd barely hit the big time before everything crashed and burned; that was the word used in the local newspapers. The people of St. Ives, especially those with invites, were buzzing about the first live performance since Jason left rehab, and even with my nerves building, I couldn't wait to see them back on stage where they belonged.

Amongst the people on the guest list were the band members' families and closest friends, a bunch of local fans the guys knew because they *always* came to their hometown shows - including Natalie the nurse. A few workers from the rehab centre also blagged invitations, and finally, members of the local press. No nationals had been invited in. Derek made it clear no videos were to be taken at the show, only photos; partly because the band wanted to keep the show on a small scale, and partly to protect me from having my stage debut posted on YouTube – a consideration I was supremely grateful for.

"Oh God." I shook my hands and jumped up and down to use up some of the nervous energy pumping through my veins. "I think I might throw up."

Lucy giggled. "Ellie, stand still. You're making *me* anxious!"

We were hiding in the toilets of the only pub in town big enough to host the event, and people wandered in and out while I bounced around like Tigger on a sugar high.

I'd learned the lyrics. Rehearsed until my throat was sore. *All that remains is doing the one thing that terrifies me.*

Put myself in front of people and risk complete humiliation.

It didn't matter that the majority of those people were family and friends, people I knew, who wouldn't judge me. That sort of made it worse. At least with random band fans, I wouldn't have to see them every day, giving me pitying glances and muttering how they'd admired my courage for putting myself out there while being secretly glad it wasn't them who'd embarrassed themselves in public.

"Lucy, I don't know about this."

"Don't. We've been through this. We've been through every single horrible possibility. We've imagined every bad thing Drew could say, and has it helped? No. It's turned you into a wreck. Ever heard of positive thinking?"

"Easy for you to say. It's hard to be positive when everything you want is resting on a song."

I'd intended to avoid Drew until the show started. Unfortunately, he was the first person I bumped into when I walked into the pub with Lucy and my parents.

He looked so good. So. Good. Ripped jeans, and a black button up shirt, sleeves rolled up to the elbows. The mix of formal and scruffy made my mouth dry out and my legs shake. I somehow choked out a hello, and I thought I saw him give me a quick once over before muttering he had to finish getting ready.

It happened again. Ache in my chest, spreading to my stomach and through my limbs until the tips of my fingers and toes throbbed with the pain of missing him.

I darted into the loos immediately after, and didn't intend to leave until the band's first song started.

"You're ready for this. You *need* to do this."

"I need to puke."

I turned to look at myself in the mirror, staring at my reflection and trying to find some internal bravery. Before I had chance to locate my inner diva, someone knocked on the door of the ladies room. Lucy and I exchanged puzzled glances, and she disappeared around the corner to see who was weird enough to knock on the door of a pub toilet before entering.

"Is she in here?"

Jason.

"Yeah, she's in here. You might as well come in, there's nobody else around."

Oh goody, it's pep talk time. I needed one. I wasn't scared enough to run away, but I began to think, if Jason wanted Drew to hear me sing, he'd have to drag him into the toilets because my feet were starting to take root right there.

When Jason laid eyes on me, he halted, staring. "Whoa."

"What?" I panicked and turned to the mirror again. "What's wrong?"

Nope No mascara down my face – surprising since I hardly ever wore the stuff. No lipstick on my teeth and my hair wasn't frizzy.

Again, Lucy giggled and Jason said, "Nothing's wrong. You look incredible."

I glanced at him over my shoulder. The thing was, I really thought I looked okay. Feeling miserable had limited my appetite, and I'd lost six pounds, making my hips a little less wide, and giving my waist a bit of definition. I'd bought new jeans - a size smaller than usual - and a close fitting black, long-sleeved top with a cowl neck. Simple, but with my hair plaited over my left shoulder and some make-up - courtesy of my little sister – I at least *appeared* confident, even if I didn't feel it.

"Thanks." I gave a weak smile while my stomach whizzed around again.

Jason took my hands, pulling me away from the mirrors. "I wanted to say something before we get started out there because if I don't do it now, the moment will pass and... well, it needs to be said."

The seriousness on his face freaked me out a bit and Lucy stepped back as if she wanted to disappear into the white tiled walls so as not to intrude.

"What is it?"

"Okay," Jason began, squeezing my hands. "I know tonight is a massive deal for you. I know you've had second thoughts every day, and I know how scared you must be. The only reason I pushed so hard for you to do this, Ellie, is because I want you to be happy. I want Drew to be happy. Every time I've messed things up for you,

you never complained. Never blamed me, and never stopped being there for me. I've been a total prick. I did some stuff I'll always be ashamed of and… you don't deserve to be miserable because I made bad choices. I'm sorry, Ellie. I was wrong to ever say you and Drew didn't make sense. You do. You make so much sense. So, if I've been a pushy asshole these past few weeks, it's because I have to make this right again. I need to do it for you. Both of you. Best friends forever, right?"

I nodded, tears threatening to smudge my make-up at the reminder of our childhood promises. I never needed an apology from Jason, not really. Sorry was only a word, after all. All I wanted was for him to get his act together and, to stop making the same mistakes over again. I knew what he was doing all along, why he pushed so hard to help me fix my relationship with Drew. Knowing he *wanted* to do it, to make up for some of the crap he put Drew and me through meant more than I could explain.

"I don't know what's going to happen tonight," he went on. "I can't predict what Drew will do or say. I'll be here whatever happens, though. And those people out there," he added, pointing towards the door, "they only want the best for you. All of them, even the ones who don't know you well. You're as much a local celebrity as the band, not because of who *we* are, but because you were flooding this town with your artwork while we were still trying to get our shit together as a group. So… shake off the nerves, okay? You can do this."

I threw my arms around Jason, unable to speak.

"Right," he said, his voice shaking slightly. "I have to get out there. Two minutes to show time."

I gave him a final squeeze, realising the next time I saw him, it would be on stage. Strangely, though, I didn't feel as sick as before. "Thank you."

Jason kissed my cheek. "Good luck, Ellie."

As he headed out, he gave Lucy a grin that made her cheeks flush. When the door closed behind him, I said, "You just fell in love with him, didn't you?"

Her face glowed more, and she lowered her head. "That was so sweet of him. I... yeah. A little bit."

A little bit *more*. I'd watched Lucy since she revealed her feelings to me, knowing at some point, she'd either get over it, or fall harder. With no idea what he'd done, with his kindness and killer smile, Jason made her fall. I couldn't stop it, she was too far gone. Instinct told me to warn her how dangerous it was to want someone like Jason; someone so unpredictable and adored, and completely wrong for her. Realism told me it would be a waste of breath. Why lecture her on what she already knew?

"Come on, Luce." I reached for her hand. "Let the madness begin!"

The pub had filled up a lot since we arrived, and we had to nudge through the crowd to our parents and Michael, who'd managed to blag one of the few available tables. Most of the tables and chairs that normally occupied space had been moved out to make way for the specially invited audience, but some remained around the edge of the room and near the bar.

"Are you okay?" Mum asked, as we sat down. She had her concerned, *we can leave if it gets too much* face on. I hadn't meant to worry her by hiding in the toilets for so long; she'd been in a constant state of worry since Drew and I broke up. It was a massive indication of how miserable I'd been, because most of the time, Mum was not a big worrier.

I nodded. "Yeah. Everything's fine."

As fine is it can be while I sit here and prepare for the most important moment of my life so far.

Not gonna lie, concentrating on the show was hard, but I listened, sang along, loved how well Jason looked, and how at home he was in front of an audience. If they hadn't already known, nobody would have guessed he almost died a few weeks ago. The memory made goose bumps pop up across my skin; the image of him in a hospital bed, hooked up to machines. Now Jason fired up the crowd as though he'd never been away. None of us could predict his future or say for sure if he'd kicked the coke for good this time. What mattered was that he was trying.

Cheers and whistles of appreciation filled the room after the last song ended. Those who had been sitting were on the their feet, and the people who'd bounced around to the entire set continued to jump, waving their arms in the air in support of their favourite band. Cameras flashed, journalists frantically scribbled notes, and I knew, right there and then, it really was the beginning for them. The guys all stepped to the front of the stage to take a bow, and it couldn't have been clearer how glad Mack and Joey were to have Jason back. Even Drew's eyes flickered with pride as chants of his brother's name filled the room. I knew if I'd asked him, he'd have insisted he was still angry with Jason and they had a long way to go before things were good between them again. It would have been true, too. But there was no disguising the genuine happiness on his face that the band was back together. Back home.

And that, right there, was the reason I fell for him. Drew could be grumpy, stubborn, unreasonable, obsessive and insecure. But he was also the man who carried me home when Jason got me stoned. The man who never had to ask what I needed; just gave it to me, sometimes before I knew myself. The man who let me hide out with him in his flat because neither of us wanted to face the world after Jason tore us both down, leaving us exhausted and broken.

The man who, although he had a million reasons to, never gave up on the things he wanted, and the people he loved.

I had no idea if I was still one of those people, but I was about to find out.

Instead of the usual dash-off-the-stage-to-avoid-the-overexcited-hordes, Jason took the mic again, his eyes swivelling towards me, silently asking if I was ready; if I was sure.

In that moment, he would have let me back out, I knew it. Because in spite of his need to fix some of the damage he'd done, he would never force me to do something I didn't want to do.

Swallowing the lump in my throat, I nodded.

"Okay, ladies and gents," Jason said, turning back to the crowd, "we're not quite finished here yet. Before I go on, I ask you to remember the no videos rule, because this gig tonight... it's for you. What happens in here stays in here. Like Vegas." A small chuckle rippled around the room, but there was no disguising the building tension. It definitely wasn't just my own, bouncing off the walls and affecting everyone. The audience whispered to each other, creating an excited buzz.

"Are you okay?" Lucy whispered, making me jump. I was trying to get *in the zone*, whatever the hell that meant. Does anyone really know what it means?

"I think so," I whispered back, and she held onto my hand as she turned her attention back to Jason.

I watched Drew looking at Mack and Joey like he was trying to figure out if they knew why Jason was still talking. They carefully avoided his gaze.

I stopped hearing Jason's words. There was only one word I needed as my cue. My name. Until then, my eyes stayed on Drew.

One thing I'd never needed help with when singing Drew's song, was emotion. Maybe it would never win any prizes for being the most lyrically beautiful song ever written, but it was *ours*. It was about us, and I felt it, every word, because I'd lived it.

I'd never had to sing it with him in the room, though. With his eyes on me while I sang the words he wrote. How could I do that? Drew was maybe six or seven feet away from me, and I'd started to shake the second I allowed myself to really look at him. Taking in the way his dark hair curled against the collar of his shirt, the sweat trickling down his cheek, his fingers still wrapped around his drumsticks as though they were a part of him the way *I* used to be a part of him.

How would it be when there was hardly any distance between us? When he was close enough to touch?

Mouth dry. Hands clammy and shaking. Heart smacking against my chest so hard it might burst out.

I flicked my head around to look at Lucy, ready to tell her I couldn't do it.

It was too late. Jason said my name, calling me to the stage.

My head was a jumbled mess, like someone had poured a tin of Alphabetti Spaghetti where my brain used to be.

"Deep breaths." Lucy stroked the back of my hand. "You can do this."

Those moments in movies, when time slows down, and everything drags across the screen, building the tension to the big money shot everyone's been waiting for.

That was my walk to the stage.

On trembling legs, I reminded myself why I *needed* to do this. I *wanted* to.

I shook my head, trying to stop the endless stream of gibberish thoughts rattling around my mind, and when I reached Jason's side, he put his arm around my shoulders to steady me.

"You okay?" he whispered as the mumbles of the crowd lessened.

"I don't know yet. I guess we'll find out together."

Behind me, shuffling feet alerted me to Mack taking his place. I wasn't sure where Joey and Jason went, and I couldn't see Drew, but I knew he hadn't left the stage. His eyes burned into my back.

Being on stage wasn't like the last time. The pub didn't have an expensive, blinding lighting system, so I could see everyone in the crowd staring at me, waiting. Natalie, stunning in a red dress, totally inappropriate for a pub gig in the middle of winter but beautiful all the same; Derek, willing me on with encouraging eyes. Then Lucy, who popped up at the front of the stage, smiling proudly, as if I was the coolest big sister in the world.

I'm not cool. I'd made a mess of everything.

The people in front of me blurred as tears flooded my eyes again.

Mack started to play, and the insanity of what I was about to do hit me full force.

Drew wrote this beautiful song for me and I broke him. Broke his trust. Broke his heart.

I was worse than Lisa. She played on his insecurities, and dropped him when he'd reached his lowest point. I swore I'd never be like her. That I'd never hurt him. I promised him I wouldn't lie to him or make him feel second best, and what did I do? The only thing guaranteed to send him spiralling back to the place in his mind where he felt like nothing.

I did that to him. And I planned to fix the mess with a reminder of everything I ruined?

I turned to Mack, holding up my hand for him to stop playing. Silence fell over the room. Not a single whisper broke through the quiet. I clung to the microphone, breathing deeply and trying not to pass out from the two hundred pairs of eyes watching me.

Lucy.

I blinked to clear my vision and found her again. She'd pushed her way to the front of the crowd, and looked up at me with a supportive smile. "Talk to him," she mouthed.

Maybe it was always that simple. Maybe all I ever needed to do was talk to him without all... *this*. It never felt like enough, though.

"Okay," I began, taking a deep breath. "I guess you're all wondering what's going on. The truth is there are only five people in this room who knew what is supposed to be happening right now. The sixth person, I'm sure, figured it out when he heard the opening to his song."

I still didn't have the strength to look at anyone other than Lucy, though. If I focused on my sister, I could forget about everyone else.

My legs were weak, ready to collapse at any second. They weren't strong enough to carry me off the stage, so I dug my heels into the floor, hoping they'd last until I'd finished... whatever I was going to say.

"The song that didn't get played is something special. Something so special, I don't think I have any right to attempt it. But the person who wrote the song... the person who writes every single Razes Hell song that gives you goose bumps, he's pretty special, too."

Closing my eyes, I breathed deeply again. Stopping the tears was impossible, so I hoped to hell nobody attempted to photograph me with make-up streaked down my face. I had to see this through to the end, whatever the consequences.

"I never thought I'd do anything like this. I never thought I'd stand in front of people and talk about private things. I'm not a celebrity. I'm Ellie. I do normal things like everyone else. I paint pictures, and hang around my flat wearing old baggy shirts and eating junk food. Sometimes I stay in my pyjamas all day, and cook weird crap from leftovers because I can't be bothered to go to the supermarket. The other very normal thing I do is fall in love." *Pause. Breathe.* "I fell in love with Drew Brooks. I didn't see it happening until I was so far gone it hurt to not be with him."

My whole body quivered, my vision blurring again as I thought about the nights I still clung to Drew's shirt, though it didn't smell like him anymore.

I wiped my eyes, and continued.

"I thought... before he knew I loved him, I thought that was the most painful thing in the world. Loving him, and being too afraid to tell him. But you know what hurts more? Knowing he's right behind me, right now, and the only reason I'm not standing beside him is because I made a stupid, horrible mistake. But even if... if this doesn't go the way I want tonight, I just... I think he deserves to know there's someone who loves him enough to... to learn a song for him and-"

There was more. So much more I wanted to say, but familiar hands touched my waist, making the rest of my words stick in my throat. My already weak legs quivered as the hands I knew so well turned me around, turning my back to the audience.

I closed my eyes. Drew cupped my face in his hands, brushing away my tears with his thumbs.

"Eleanor Jane," he said, his voice husky. "What am I going to do with you?"

My heart hammered so fast I could hardly breathe. Instead of speaking, I let myself get lost in the gentle movements of his fingers over my cheeks, drying each droplet of moisture that fell.

"Look at me."

I shook my head. *Still not ready.*

Drew's lips planted soft kisses on my eyelids, causing flutters in my stomach. "Look. At. Me."

"I can't," I whispered.

"No?" His stubble lightly brushed my cheek, making my heart beat harder. "I think the girl who told a room full of people how much she loves someone can do anything she wants to."

I didn't feel anywhere near as brave as he made me sound, but it was easier to fake when he held me.

Everything was easier with him.

Slowly, I lifted my eyelids, and he smiled though his own eyes were glistening. "There's my girl."

"Drew-"

"Wait."

Without any warning, he swept me off the ground, and the crowd – who I'd completely forgotten about – gave a loud cheer as Drew walked off the stage with me in his arms.

He carried me outside, placing me back on my feet in front the pub's doors. The cold hit me immediately. My internal organs were on pause, waiting for Drew to speak. He stood in front of me, not touching me, just watching me with awe.

"I can't believe you did that for me. You... you were going to sing your song."

I nodded, my body relaxing a little. "I practised. A lot. I'm sorry I couldn't do it, Drew. I ... it felt wrong, like I was using the words you wrote to make you feel guilty or something, and-"

Drew's mouth closed over mine, putting a stop to my panicked rambling. His kiss was life being breathed back into me. Everything inside me that had been dead and listless began to stir and awaken.

"Ells, it was an amazing thing for you to attempt." He rested one hand on my hip while the other gently played with the ends of my hair. "I'm sorry I made you think you had to do something so big to get me to listen." He shook his head, his eyes glistening again. "I wanted to talk to you every day. Every time I saw you, I felt like my guts were being ripped out all over again, not because of what you did, but because I left you. In the hospital, I left you there, begging me to listen. I walked away. I didn't think... I thought you'd never forgive me for leaving you there."

The memory of the most painful moment of my life forced more tears to spill; when he prised my fingers from his arm and turned his back on me.

"I didn't blame you for reacting the way you did. I lied to you. I confirmed every fear you had about me and Jason, but it wasn't because I-"

"I know, Ells." Drew rested his forehead against mine. "I get that it wasn't about you having a thing for him. And I didn't want to stop you being close to him, I just wanted to feel as though I meant more, and I should have already known. I *did* mean more."

"You *do*." I stepped forward to close the gap between us. A happy sigh escaped my lips as I nestled into his chest, snuggling into his warmth.

"How did you find out about your song, Ells?"

"How do you think?"

Drew held me tighter, slipping both arms around me. "Jason."

"Yes. Jason."

"He did this for us."

"Yup. He never does anything on a small scale."

"For sure." I looked up, and saw Drew staring thoughtfully over my shoulder. "Things with me and Jason aren't much better, Ellie. But we're trying. *I'm* trying." He paused then fixed his gaze on me. "I don't ever want to make you think I'm not listening or that you can't be around for Jason without me flipping out. He needs you too. More than you know. I don't want to get in the way of your friendship with him. What you said in there made me feel like an arse for not seeing things clearly before now. For not understanding what you told me every day we were together." Drew paused again. "I can't promise to always do everything right, but I promise to try. I need to be with you, Ells. I love you."

The words I'd missed so much danced through my brain, and I let them hang in the air between us. I thought I would never hear them again.

"I don't need you to do everything right. I need you to be you. That's all I ever wanted."

All I'll ever want.

I reached up on my tiptoes and wound my arms around his neck. "I love you too."

When Drew's lips found mine, I knew we were going to be okay. His arms were my home, his body was my shelter, and his kiss re-lit a spark in me that had never fully fizzled out, not even when we were apart.

Maybe nobody ever knows for sure how life will turn out, but in that moment, *I* knew I was where I'd always wanted to be. The little girl on the lonely step, holding on to the little boy who didn't know who he was yet.

Want more rock star romances?

Check out *Blurring The Lines* by Mia Josephs

Christian Meyer quit his band and checked into rehab. Only, when he checks out to start his solo career, he can't write. At all.

Corinne's done the Hollywood, famous rockstar boyfriend thing. It ended in such a huge disaster that she ran herself out of town, despite her career as a songwriter just beginning to take off. She lives in a small cabin in the woods of Washington to keep as far away from her old life as possible.

But when Christian is desperate to start his new career, and his manager has the perfect songwriter in mind, their worlds collide.

Corinne is determined to keep her distance, it's just collaborating for a weekend. But when Chris shows up on her doorstep weeks after their meeting and pleading for help, she can't turn him away.

With the life she now lives and the past she's desperate to keep buried, she'll do everything she can to protect her heart, no matter how quickly she feels herself falling.

For the first time in his life, Chris can see himself being in love, but with a tour date looming, and Corinne terrified to move forward, they both have a long road to travel if there's a chance of them being together.

About The Author

Kyra Lennon is a self-confessed book-a-holic, and has been since she first learned to read. When she's not reading, you'll usually find her hanging out in coffee shops with her trusty laptop and/or her friends, or girling it up at the nearest shopping mall.
Kyra grew up on the South Coast of England and refuses to move away from the seaside which provides massive inspiration for her novels.

To find out more about Kyra, check out her blog, website, follow her on Twitter, Facebook or Pinterest, or drop her an email at kyralennon@gmail.com

Also by Kyra Lennon

The Game On Series

Game On (Game On Book 1)
Praise for *Game On*

"Loved this book! Radleigh might be loathsome, but he's magnetic! Kyra has a witty style and excellent character development." - Elizabeth Seckman, Author of *Past Due*

"Game On is a moving, emotional, very real contemporary romance filled with fun, friendship, laughter, and a look on the human condition." - Clare Dugmore, Writer

Blindsided (Game On Book 2)
Praise for *Blindsided*

"Once again, Kyra Lennon has brought some fantastic characters to life, and as with Taylor in Game On *she hasn't shied away from a love-to-hate character Mischa."* - Annalisa Crawford, Author of *Cat and The Dreamer* and *That Sadie Thing*

"I absolutely loved this book! It was such an easy read, had it done in two sittings, and the love story was so cute and sweet. I think it was a perfect fit for Jesse, because he deserves this kind of love story." - Becca Ann, Author of *Reasons I Fell For The Funny Fat Friend*

Sidelined (Game On Book 3)
Praise for *Sidelined*

"I've always loved Kyra's no-mess writing style. She lets you into her character's heads that it didn't matter what the clothes they wore looked like, or where they lived, how they sat, and all those details that tend to get overdone at times. I pictured everything because those characters felt so real to me it's like I could call Bree up on the phone and beg her to take me shopping." - Cassie Mae, Author of *How To Date A Nerd* and *Switched*

"It goes without saying Kyra Lennon is a fantastic writer. She manages to keep an intricate plot exciting and fresh." - Confessions of a YA and NA Book Addict

If I Let You Go
Praise for *If I Let You Go*

"This is an amazing contemporary romance novella that makes you giggle, cry, and swoon. It has powerful cast of characters and a clean modern style. I highly recommend If I Let You Go *to anyone who loves a good love story."* – Christine Rains, Author of Fearless

"With a fast-paced plot and relatable characters, Kyra Lennon's If I Let You Go *is a must read."* - Cherie Reich, Author of the Gravity series

Printed in Great Britain
by Amazon.co.uk, Ltd.,
Marston Gate.